TAKEN

A Kept Novella

Sally Bradley

To those who've stood for right,
when right was labeled as wrong.

CHAPTER ONE

"Cameron, it's... me."

Her hushed words on his voicemail still silenced his breathing, even years after hearing her new greeting for the first time. Ever since they'd reunited, those three words and that scared yet bold pause between them always made him stand motionless, hold his breath, and wonder.

Wonder if she regretted what she'd done.

Of course not, she'd say.

If her life might ever be normal.

Cameron, this is *my normal.*

If wrong would someday be made right.

Cam Winters smiled sadly at his phone, the screen fading to black. He tucked it into his pocket and moved forward with his day.

That last question? That one he couldn't quite stomach.

Because the answer was *no*. It could never be made right.

"Ah. Those two…" Jordan Foster's voice was wistful, a mix of happiness and melancholy, as her brother's car drove away.

Walking beside her away from Chicago's Buckingham Fountain, Cam turned his gaze from his best friend's car to study his best friend's sister. What made her sound so sad?

She met his gaze, her brown eyes matching the hair that framed her pretty face, and smiled at him. "Dillan and Miska are engaged—finally. But now we've got to wait for the wedding."

"Won't be long, by the sounds of it." Cam stopped at a crosswalk while traffic zoomed by. Dillan getting married. He'd begun to think the guy would be single forever. Which was probably the same thing people thought about him, older than Dillan and still single at thirty-two.

"I'm glad Dillan asked us to videotape him proposing, you know?" Jordan hugged herself, all wistfulness gone. "Wasn't that the most romantic thing? Taking her to all the spots by Buckingham Fountain that had connected them? Then him taking her to a new spot to actually propose? Creating a new memory here?"

Yep. It was romantic. Had to give Dillan credit for that. Cam pretended deep interest in the sun-lit skyline in front of him. "Dillan's gone soft."

"Gone soft?" Jordan's mouth fell open, and she whacked his shoulder with the back of her fist.

Cam laughed.

"Being romantic does not mean a guy's gone soft. It means… he's a real man."

"Ah, Jordan. You're cute."

"I should have known that'd be news to you."

"What? That you're cute?"

She rolled her eyes. "That real men are romantic."

He snorted, warming up to their banter. "I can be romantic."

"That's not what I hear."

"Yeah? From whom?"

She raised her chin and tossed her hair over her shoulder.

But now he wanted to know. "Come on, Jordan. Who says that?"

She faced him again, flirtatiously tilting up her nose. "Everyone."

"I have not dated everyone. That's not even a valid answer."

"Puh-lease."

"For example. You. I have not dated you."

Her teasing look morphed into seriousness.

She was supposed to laugh at that. Keep the joke going. If she knew the feelings he'd been fighting about her… He swallowed. "I have definitely not dated everyone." How had this conversation happened? This was Dillan's sister, after all. His twenty-two-year-old sister. Cam's best friend's much younger sister whom he'd wanted to date for a year now. But of course she was off limits because of…

Yeah. All of that.

The walk sign flashed—mercifully—and he gestured

across the street. "Let's go."

She walked beside him, long legs matching his pace, hand swinging so close to his.

He made a fist, then spread his fingers. Why did he have to point out that he'd never dated her? And why did she have to react that way?

And why was Dillan the lucky guy who'd found his girl?

They headed for his car, parked several car lengths ahead. Cam cleared his throat. "That is some pretty stellar parallel parking there, if you ask me."

"Is that why you quit dating girls after a few weeks? Because you don't know how to be romantic?"

The highway had better be empty so it wouldn't take long to get her home. "Seriously. Look at how close those tires are to the curb."

"Cam, you seem uncomfortable talking about this."

Smart aleck. "I'm totally fine talking about my parallel parking skills."

She pulled him to a stop beside a car that wasn't parked nearly as well. "But not relationships. Which never last with you. Why?"

He tried to send her a patient, fatherly smile. "Jordan…"

She sent the smile back. "Cam."

All right then. If she wanted to talk about it, he'd talk about it. "First of all, I don't keep dating someone if it's not going to work out. I'd call that being a good guy, maybe. Second…"

She tilted her head and that soft, thick brown hair slid over her shoulder.

What was his second point?

"Go on," she said.

"Umm…" Had he even had a second point? "I haven't dated anyone this year."

"Five whole months. Wow. What's your reason?"

She was teasing him; he could hear it in her voice. But he couldn't answer, because *she* was the reason. She'd been about to graduate from college and come home for good.

No, he definitely couldn't tell her that over the last few years, as he and Dillan had become good friends, Cam had gotten to know her too, and liked—loved?—everything he'd seen. Time to find a much safer topic of conversation. "You found a job yet?"

"Still looking. Is five months a record for you?"

"No. Once I didn't date for a number of years."

Her eyebrows rose in surprise.

"Yeah, from age zero to thirteen. Didn't date once."

"Oh, Cam." She closed her eyes, shook her head. "How you must have suffered."

He chuckled as they reached his silver Altima. They slid inside and Cam started the engine, then waited for an opening in traffic.

They'd left downtown behind them before Jordan spoke again. "What are you going to do, now that Dillan's getting married?"

"I am going to drop you off at home, then probably stop at Portillo's on *my* way home to pick up a couple hot dogs."

"You are so exasperating."

Yeah, he kinda was, wasn't he?

"Would you ever date a friend's sister?"

What? Cam focused on the cop ahead who kept him

from being able to speed home and drop this woman off. Why would she ask him that? He wracked his brain for another woman in the church's singles group who had a brother he was friends with.

He couldn't come up with one.

Was she referring to herself?

"Cam?"

"Jordan."

She huffed in frustration. "What is up with you? You've been shutting down on me ever since Dillan and Miska left."

Was this how twenty-two-year-olds were now? This clueless and persistent? "Jordan, has it occurred to you that this might be an awkward conversation?"

"Why? Because you want to ask me out?"

He stared at the back of the Escalade in front of him, at the taillights flashing red—

Cam slammed on his brakes, coming close to rear-ending the SUV.

A sudden jam of traffic formed around them, everyone sitting on their brakes.

Of all the times to have no distraction to claim.

He made himself face her.

She watched him, vulnerability on her own features, in those big eyes, across her mouth.

Cam blinked back up at her eyes. Was she really saying that she was interested in him?

He'd wondered last week, after spending Memorial Day at the zoo with her and Miska and Dillan. Miska and Dillan had hung back, caught up in each other, which gave him hours with Jordan. He'd loved every second with her—but she was off limits. Plus, he was too old for her. He was kidding himself, longing to see interest.

"Do you?" she asked.

He squinted. Did he what?

"Want to ask me out?"

He wet his lips and looked back at the road. What would Dillan say? To him? To Jordan? "Why would you ask that?"

"Because we've practically been double-dating with Dillan and Miska since I got home from school. We've spent a lot of time together, and I thought…"

Silence fell. Cam glanced at his rearview mirror.

Traffic piled up behind them. Ahead, no one moved. They were going to be here awhile.

"Jordan, I find it very ironic that traffic stops the moment you ask that question."

She kept her head turned just enough that he couldn't see past all her dark hair. "Why's that?"

Because he did want, so much, to date her. Wanted it more every time he was with her.

It had driven him crazy all last week.

"Jordan—" His voice gave out. What should he say?

A smile crept across her lips. "So I was right—you *are* interested."

Denying it—when it was the truth and evidently way more obvious than he'd meant it to be—would only hurt her. He couldn't do it. But he couldn't speak either.

"Are you worried about Dillan?" she asked.

"Dillan *and* Garrett. Your dad. Any other male relatives you have."

She laughed and twisted in her seat to face him better. "Dillan's okay with it."

That caught him off guard. "Wait a second. You've talked to Dillan about… this?"

She laughed at him again. "Of course. Why do you think we've been together so much lately?"

Dillan had been setting him up? With his sister? His ten-years-younger sister? "Jordan…" He let his head fall back against the headrest. "I admit it; I'd love to date you. But we're ten years apart."

"Nine years and ten months."

"Dillan might be okay with this, but—"

"And six days."

He nodded. Like that made a difference. "Your dad will try to kill me. Then ground you."

"I'm twenty-two, Cam."

"Again. Exactly."

This time she had no comeback, only held his gaze like she really didn't care that he might die—or lose a limb, neck, head—by asking her out.

"None of that phases you? You really think your dad's going to be okay with it?"

She shrugged. "Sure. He knows you."

"Some."

"He knows you and Dillan are good friends. That's a plus on your side."

Cam grunted.

"And as long as you don't jerk me around like Matt did, he'll let you live."

At the mention of her previous on-again, off-again

boyfriend, Cam stilled. "That's over? For good?"

"It is." Her smile vanished, but she didn't look sorry about the situation. "Cam, I'm a twenty-two-year-old woman—"

He was very aware of that.

"—who wants to find the right man. The man God wants for me. I'm not looking for a good time or some guy to fill a boyfriend role. I want real love. Marriage. A family."

Family. One of the main reasons he'd kept women at arms' length for so long. Cam studied her. He knew Jordan. She wasn't playing him, wasn't making up some story just to use him. She meant all of that.

Plus she was safe. Dependable. Smart. In time, he probably could trust her with… everything.

He let the smallest smile break through. "I don't know, Jordan. You're pretty forward. Back in my day, a girl would never—"

"They would too, and you know it."

He laughed.

She held her lower lip between her teeth, something bright and happy shining in her eyes.

Cam returned the look, setting her smile free.

"So?" she finally asked.

He shifted in his seat, planted his palm on top of her headrest. "So, Miss Foster, if your brothers and your dad let me live, would you be interested in dating an old dude like me?"

She scrunched her shoulders together, looking like a college co-ed again. "I'd love to, Cam."

He leaned a bit over the console between them. "No,

this is where you stroke my ego and tell me I'm not old."

She leaned a little closer. "Cam?" she whispered.

Oh, she was beautiful. His gaze roamed her face. "Yeah?"

"Tell me again what it was like before indoor plumbing."

This was it. Had to be. He knelt in front of the updated, eighties-era, side-split house and tied his shoe. Slowly. Didn't look like anyone was home, but he'd wait on the street leading into this cul-de-sac and watch. He knew what the guy—this Cameron John Winters—looked like. If he lived here, eventually he'd have to drive by.

Eventually he'd see who owned this home. See if he'd tracked the right guy. Found the right name.

And when he was certain and could tell his client that the man he was looking for owned this home, they'd be that much closer to the real target, the one his client had been searching for for years.

The one who, for so long, Winters had been hiding.

CHAPTER TWO

By the time they left the interstate, Jordan had convinced Cam to spend the rest of the day with her and her family, waiting for Dillan and Miska to return to celebrate their engagement.

Cam needed to stop by his house for some things, so forty minutes later he pulled into the driveway of his home, the front a mix of soft-red brick and white siding. He parked in the driveway and sent her a smile that hinted at timidity. "You ready?"

She'd never been to his house, which was understandable since it wasn't close to her parents' home. She returned his smile, forcing complete confidence into hers. "Let's get your stuff." Once out of the car, she followed him up the concrete drive and half-dozen steps to his front door.

He unlocked it and pushed it open for her, letting her go in first.

Jordan walked into a large, simple living room, stairs on her right going up a half level and down another half level. The hardwood floors boasted a dark stain, and the gray sectional sofa and massive flat screen filled one half of the spacious room. Beyond them sat two overstuffed chairs with an end table and lamp between them.

She faced him as he locked the door behind them. "This is nice. You remodeled all of this?"

"Gutted it." He scanned the room, hands on his hips, then flashed her a grin. "This room is clean, but I don't remember what state my kitchen's in. Wait here."

"Cam—"

"Nope." He held up a hand as he walked past her, laughing. "Got to make sure I'm making a good impression."

"Fine." She drew the word out. "I'll humor you."

He disappeared around the living room wall, and in seconds the sounds of the dishwasher filling reached her.

Smiling, Jordan shook her head. She wandered toward the sectional. "How long have you lived here?"

"Uh, four years, I think."

She searched the walls and end tables for pictures. Nothing. "Did you decorate this place yourself?"

"What?" he called over clanking glass.

She turned to face the wall that held the coat closet and ascending staircase. "I said did you decorate—"

A teddy bear on the bottom step cut off her words.

"Did I decorate? Yeah. I guess you'd call it decorating."

Jordan took a step closer.

A well-worn, white bear with black eyes and paws. And beneath it, two Matchbox cars.

"I mean, I bet it looks pretty sterile to you. But it works for me. What does a guy need more than a big couch and TV, right?"

Why did he have toys on his stairs? Especially looking like they'd been left there for someone to carry upstairs and put away?

"Jordan?"

The running water in the kitchen quieted, and Jordan spun toward the couch, her back to the stairs. If he had toys, well, that was… odd. And if he knew she'd seen them, things could get really, really awkward.

There had to be some explanation.

She ran a finger along the couch cushion's seam as Cam reappeared.

"It's pretty plain, isn't it?" he asked.

She crossed her arms, then pressed a finger against her lips. "Nothing a few throw pillows and art wouldn't fix." Maybe.

He stood beside her and nodded. "I guess." He glanced her way. "Ready to see the kitchen?"

Maybe he collected Matchbox cars. Guys did that, didn't they? She prayed her smile looked natural. "Lead the way."

The kitchen made her momentarily forget the toys. The upper cabinets were a winter white, the lowers gray and topped with what looked like marble countertops. The backsplash boasted a marble, chevroned pattern that tied it all together. A teal teapot sat on the back burner of a six-burner, stainless steel range.

"Wow. You did this?"

"Mostly." He crossed his arms over his chest, satisfaction in his stance. "I hired a designer to get the layout and design right, but I did the tiling. Helped with the cabinet install. Put in the lights."

She glanced up at the recessed lighting above. "You're good."

"Thank you." He relaxed his arms. "I'll get my laptop, then we'll go."

"Okay."

He headed for the stairs.

"Mind if I get a glass of water?" she called after him.

"Sure." His words came from partway up the stairs. "Glasses are above the dishwasher."

She found the cabinet and opened it. Half a dozen tall, glass glasses stood on the right side. She reached for one.

On the left side sat a stack of small, plastic cups.

Her hand halted a fingertip away from a glass.

Cups with Disney princes and princesses. Cups with Dora the Explorer...

Cups for children.

Huh.

Cam's footsteps sounded upstairs.

Jordan grabbed an adult glass and crossed to the stainless steel fridge, filling it there. She stayed in front of the refrigerator as she drank and scanned the pictures across the front. She'd just enjoy pictures of Cam and forget everything odd she'd seen.

She smiled at a picture of him with her brothers after doing some run together. Cam wasn't short, but he did look a little short next to her two giants of brothers, both well over six feet tall. Cam was definitely the best looking of the bunch, though. His brown hair wasn't as dark as hers, and he wasn't as lean as Dillan and Garrett, but he sure had the best smile. The nicest eyes.

After a lifetime being around such tall men, dating someone closer to her own height sounded wonderful.

Most of the other pictures held familiar faces. Cam with guys from the church's singles group. Pictures from last year's Memorial Day party. From a winter day spent downtown. From the Fourth of July.

Funny—she'd never thought a guy would put up pictures like this. Especially pictures of friends from church. Where were the pictures of his family?

She scanned a couple more that included people she knew until she came to one with Cam holding a young girl in his arms, a smiling brown-haired woman beside him, her hand wrapped around his upper arm. Like he belonged to her. To the little girl.

To them.

Cam started down the stairs.

Jordan took another swallow and studied the picture more closely.

The girl—did she have Down Syndrome?

Yes, it looked like it.

She studied Cam's face.

The picture seemed fairly recent. Maybe a year or so old. Who was this girl? This woman? Where did they fit with Cam? Were they family?

Or something else?

He entered the kitchen and set his laptop on the island. "Ready to go?"

"Sure." She dragged her gaze from the picture to him.

Cam stood still, his own gaze stuck on the picture, looking as if he wished she hadn't seen it.

Why? She looked back at it, praying her voice would sound nonchalant. "Who's this?"

"Just…" It sounded like he swallowed. "Someone close to me."

The little girl held the teddy bear she'd seen on the stairs.

Jordan caught her breath. What did this mean? Nothing? Something?

Everything?

She faced him again, not faking a thing this time. "How close, Cam?"

Somehow, the question softened him. "Very close, Jordan."

"That doesn't make me…" Should she be honest? She pushed her bangs to the side. She'd played the game with Matt, waiting and wondering, never being bold enough to ask where she stood or why he couldn't commit. No, she was done with that dance. It was time to be bold. "I don't know if I like that."

Slowly, he walked to her, his hands in his pockets. He looked at the picture, then back at her. "I can't explain her to you now, Jordan. Someday I hope to. But for now I need you to trust me."

Though his words were vague, Jordan clung to the promise beneath them. She took a deep breath. The woman, the girl, the bear, the cups … "Okay. I'll trust you."

"Thank you." His brown eyes searched hers, warmth coming from them. "That means a lot."

Good. It should.

He held a hand toward his living room. "You ready to go?"

"Sure."

She set the drink aside while he tucked his laptop under his arm and led the way to the front door.

But as they passed the staircase, Jordan couldn't help looking for the teddy bear and toy cars.

The staircase was empty.

Before dialing his client, he waited until the silver Altima drove by and turned at the intersection.

"Yes?" the man said, never one for *hello*.

"I found him."

Something creaked in the background. "Really. What's his name?"

"Cameron Winters."

"Cameron Winters." Silence held for a few moments. "Then we're looking for a Hannah Winters."

"That would be my guess."

"You found her yet?"

"No, but I'm on his street and he just left with a woman."

"Hannah?" Excitement colored the client's tone.

"No. Younger. Darker hair."

"Maybe she knows where Hannah is."

"Maybe. I wouldn't know."

"You will."

"Of course." That went without saying. He started his engine and followed the path the Altima had taken. "Now that I know his name, I can start looking for her under her maiden name. Give me a few days, and I'll have more information."

"I want it faster than that, Thomas."

Impatient, arrogant clients were the worst. "I'll get the info when I get it, and not before."

The man grunted. "Fine. Just... I need to find Hannah."

"And we'll find her. If we have the right man, Winters will lead us to her."

CHAPTER THREE

The afternoon could not have gone better.

Sure, there'd initially been some tension after Jordan saw Anna's picture and he hadn't been able to talk about it, but lunch together at her favorite Mexican restaurant eventually fixed that. By the time they left, two hours and one big tip later, it felt like everything was right between them again.

It felt so right being with Jordan, like she really was the woman he could spend his life with. The woman he could grow old with.

The woman he could trust Anna and Sophie with.

When they finally headed to Jordan's parents' house, it was almost time for dinner. Dillan and Miska arrived at the same time, and Jordan oohed and ahhed over Miska's ring.

Jordan's other brother, Garrett, was already there, and it seemed to take a good ten minutes to get everyone out of the foyer, what with all the hugs and congratulations and women gushing and everything.

Shari, Jordan's mom, had cooked a special meal to celebrate the engagement. Seated at the table next to Jordan and across from Dillan, Cam felt like one of the family. Like a part of one of the best families he knew.

How much he wanted a life like this.

After dinner, he hooked his laptop up to the Fosters' TV and, again, seated himself beside Jordan as they watched the video he'd recorded of the proposal. There wasn't much audio to speak of since he and Jordan were too far from the couple to pick up sound, but the video had caught little bits of Jordan's excited whisperings, her barely contained squeal when Dillan had dropped to one knee, and a few deep chuckles from Cam.

And of course, it had also captured all the romance of a couple getting engaged.

Cam glanced at Dillan and Miska seated close together on the couch, Dillan's arm around her, his fingers stroking her shoulder. He couldn't stop smiling, glancing from time to time at Miska who couldn't stop watching the rerun of their engagement.

Across the room, Shari wiped tears from her eyes, and her husband squeezed her hand. Even Garrett, the one who always had a joke for everything, seemed happy with the day's event.

Would they react the same if it was him and Jordan getting engaged?

The depth of how much he hoped so surprised him. How had he fallen so fast for Jordan? Could he be this certain this quickly? What if he told her too much and then she ended up not being the one?

Could he risk telling her everything? Putting Anna and Sophie—and even himself—at risk?

The video ended, and Jordan squeezed his arm. "That

was so great. I want to see it again."

Heaving a dramatic sigh, Garrett pushed himself up off a recliner. "You girls watch it to your heart's content. I say us guys need to shoot some hoops."

Like Cam ever had a chance to win, playing against two guys that tall. "Why do you always want to play basketball when I'm here?" he asked.

Garrett grinned, as if he'd read Cam's mind. "Dillan, you in?"

"What?" Dillan looked up from where he still sat, deep in conversation with Miska.

Cam stood. "Actually, I need to head home."

Jordan linked her fingers through his. "Already?"

Garrett and Dillan straightened. Eyed him.

Suddenly it felt a bit hot and crowded in the living room. "Yeah, I need to go. Got some things to take care of tonight." Anna might be home soon, and she'd probably need some sort of help. Emotional help. Either she or the kids.

Garrett crossed his arms, cocked his head, and narrowed his eyes, but his mouth tightened as if he was fighting a smile.

Didn't Jordan see that? Cam let go of her hand. "Thanks for letting me crash the Foster party." He offered Dillan a hand. "Congrats again, man."

Dillan shook his hand but looked between him and his sister. "Thanks. Glad you were here."

Jordan's fingers settled around his arm. "I'll walk you out."

So she *was* trying to get him killed. "All right."

He said his goodbyes to Miska, to Jordan's parents, and a now openly smirking Garrett and followed Jordan to the foyer.

She paused before the front door and smiled up at him. "Today was great, Cam."

Yeah, it was. Except for the last thirty seconds maybe. He pushed that uncomfortableness away and took in the sight of the woman he'd fallen for. "Thanks for spending it with me."

"Anytime. And thanks for hanging out with my family. Everyone loves you, you know."

No. They only *liked* what they knew about him. His smile faded, and he couldn't help running a hand through his hair, glancing around the small entryway for something to say. "Jordan…"

Why did it always come back to the secrets he'd kept? The things he regretted? To events he couldn't change?

Jordan's eyes held no worries, no confusion. Just confidence.

Because she was so young and innocent.

She didn't know his story. Didn't know his family's saga. Didn't know the damage done, the trouble they'd been in. Her family was perfect—just about. Could she really understand what had made him *him?*

"I don't come from this." He flipped his hand out, gesturing to the space around him. "Your family, Jordan… They're great, but I can't give you this."

"What do you mean?" She stepped closer. "Give me what? I'm not following."

"Your parents are wonderful. You've got this close-knit

family that loves each other. I've got…" A mess.

"Have you forgotten about Miska? About Garrett?" she asked, clearly referring to the less-than-perfect pasts they'd come from.

"It isn't like that, Jordan."

She tipped her head, gave him an *are-you-serious* glare.

"Look, I'm being honest with you. I like you… way too much. But there are things I haven't told anybody. Things I *can't* tell anybody."

"Why not?"

She wasn't even trying to understand, was she? Which showed how black and white her world was. "Because it's not safe to, Jordan."

"You're not making sense."

He probably wasn't, not to her. "I don't know if this is a good idea—"

She laughed incredulously. "Are you serious? You're worse than Matt, Cam! At least we'd date for a few months before he'd disappear. You didn't even make it through the day."

"Hey. Stop it. That's not what this is."

"Really?" Her eyes shone. "You're not ending things between us? Because that's exactly what it sounds like."

"There's nothing to end, Jordan. We haven't started."

She jerked open the front door. "Good. Then leave."

"No." This whole conversation had just gone insane. "You're blowing this out of proportion. You're not listening to me."

"No, I'm listening. You've spent a morning and an afternoon with me, and you're chickening out." Her voice quivered, the anger that had colored it gone. "I'm so tired of guys being like this. Playing me, jerking me one way and then the other."

"I'm not playing you," he growled.

"Then what are you doing?"

Her question stumped him. He was doing the same thing he always did—protecting the woman he was dating. Keeping her at a distance, just in case the past came back to haunt him.

Like before, the wall he put up would cost him a relationship, love, a new family.

He couldn't lose Jordan. But how could he tell her everything? It wasn't his call to make.

Dillan came around the corner from the living room, a grin on his face. "I hope I'm not interrupting, but Garrett thinks you two are—"

"Just saying goodbye." Jordan's voice was firm. Final. "See you at church, Cam."

"You said you'd trust me," he reminded her.

"And then you pulled a Matt. 'Bye, Cam." She pulled the door open even wider and gestured for him to leave.

Cam looked at Dillan for help, but Dillan's face only registered surprise and confusion as he stared at his sister.

Once again, Cam had made a mess of it. And in record time too. As much as he wanted to stay and fight, he couldn't. Not yet. He nodded goodnight to Jordan, then to Dillan. "See you guys tomorrow." He stepped through the doorway.

The door closed, loudly, behind him.

Cam halted on the sidewalk, tempted to turn around

and tell her to quit throwing a fit. But this wasn't the right time or place. Not when they were celebrating Dillan and Miska's engagement. Jordan needed an evening to cool off.

And he needed time to think. To figure out how to be open with a woman when he couldn't even talk about the majority of his life.

Basically, he needed a miracle.

CHAPTER FOUR

Anna was already home when Cam pulled into his driveway. Her car was tucked in the garage, out of sight like always, but the front door was open, the screen door offering a peek into the entryway.

When he walked through the door, the sound of Anna cleaning the kitchen met him—the clank of a pot in the sink and the steady splash of running water. He tossed his keys onto the console table by the coat closet and followed the sounds.

She was looking over her shoulder at the doorway when he entered, her hand clenched around a metal sauce pan. Her grip relaxed, and she smiled at him. "Hey. How are you?"

"I'm okay." He eased onto a stool on the other side of the island. He felt old. Old, tired, weary. "How are you all?"

"Hanging in there."

"How's Sophie?"

"The same." She rinsed the pan and set it on top of a stack of other clean dishes in the dish drain. "If it's okay with you, I'd like to head back. Spend the night with her."

Which meant he might not make it to church tomorrow. Wouldn't get to see Jordan. What timing. He ran a hand down the back of his neck. "Sure."

She dried her hands on the towel on the oven rail and tightened her ponytail, studying him the entire time. "Cameron? What's going on?"

He rested his elbow on the island top, ran his thumb across his lip, and stared past her, out the kitchen window into the backyard.

Avery and Logan chased each other across the grass, hidden by the high walls of his privacy fence.

What he wouldn't give to have a whole family. To have a wife he loved, who loved him back. To have his own kids filling the extra bedrooms in his house—the bedrooms Avery, Logan, and Anna now filled.

Anna interrupted his thoughts. "What happened with Jordan today?"

"Her brother got engaged."

"Your friend? Dillan?"

Cam nodded.

"And Jordan?"

He met Anna's eyes. "She wanted to date me."

"That's great."

"*Wanted.* Past tense." He sighed. "I brought her here today. Just for a few minutes. She saw your picture. Yours and Sophie's."

Anna glanced at the fridge, then back at him. "What happened?"

"The same thing that always happens. I can't tell her anything—except she took it wrong and got mad at me.

Thought I was ending things."

"Are you going to let her go?"

"No." The word came without thought, but once it was free, he didn't try to take it back. "No. I feel like she's the one for me. I've spent these years getting to know her, and then this past month since she's been home…"

"So tell her."

The simple sentence shocked him. He could only blink Anna's way. "Tell her?"

"About us. About everything. You knew, Cameron, that someday there'd be a woman worth sharing it with."

She sounded so sure. "You've never met her."

"You've told me everything I need to know. Plus you're different when you talk about her. She matters. A lot."

She did. "You sure I should tell her? You're the one with the most at stake."

Anna shook her head. "You're not losing this one because of me. You tell her. And if you want me here when you tell her, I'll be here."

Just that quickly, the weariness of loss lifted from him.

Anna had never talked like this before. She'd always been so full of fear, always watching over her shoulder. Always hiding.

"What if…" he started.

"What?"

"What if she doesn't take it well?" Why was he still grasping at reasons to hold back? Jordan might be young but she was solid. Mature. Their story wouldn't freak her out.

"Pray about it, Cameron. Ask God to guide you. But if

you're asking me, I've heard enough to know that there's something special about this girl."

There absolutely was.

Anna pushed away from the island. "Have you eaten?"

"Yeah. You guys?"

"Just finished. Can you make sure Avery and Logan get their baths tonight?"

What a woman Anna was, carrying such a heavy load. And now she was freeing him to go after the woman he… well, loved. "We'll be good here, Anna. Go take care of Sophie."

She kissed him on the cheek as she passed by.

"Jordan."

Cam's voice behind her made her falter, her shoulder bumping the auditorium door as she left the church service Sunday morning. She turned.

He was a few people behind her, quickly making his way through them to her.

He hadn't been at Sunday School that morning—which had surprised her, honestly. For almost as long as she'd known him, he'd been known as the guy who dated the new girl for a few weeks, then ended it. But he'd never not shown up the Sunday after a breakup. Where had he been today?

He stopped in front of her, closer than she expected. "Hey," he said, his voice low and serious. "You got a minute?"

He thought whatever they had to talk about would only take a minute? Should she be insulted or relieved? "I guess."

He reached for her arm, then caught himself and motioned to the side of the foyer.

Jordan followed him. "You missed Pastor announcing Dillan and Miska's engagement."

"Yeah, I couldn't…" His words fell flat again, like he was struggling over each one. "I couldn't get away when I wanted to."

Okay. She had no idea what to say to that. To any of this.

"Can I apologize?" he said. "For how everything ended yesterday? I just started saying the stuff I normally do, and I wasn't thinking about how it would come across to you. I'm sorry for that."

An apology was nice, but what did it change? "Thank you."

"I've thought about yesterday a lot." He swallowed and looked down at his hands, scowled at them. "About the things I wanted to say to you but didn't think I could. About things going on in my world, things nobody here knows about…"

Cam and his secrets. She and Miska had talked about him last night after he'd left, about how whatever was in his past had to be something big for him to still keep from addressing it. "Are you ever going to share it with anyone?"

He met her gaze, his hazel eyes deep and somber. "I'd like to tell you."

His words stilled her.

"You asked about that picture on my fridge. And I told

you I wanted to tell you someday. If you're still interested in hearing it, I think the time has come."

So quickly? How had *someday* become the next day? "Who is she?"

He lowered his voice. "She's my sister."

Why was that such a secret? "And the little girl?"

He cleared his throat. "My niece."

"She has Down Syndrome?"

He nodded.

"Why the big secret? Are you ashamed of her?"

"No." His response was quiet but filled with frustration. "Sophie's the best—" He glanced around the foyer, then back at her. "Jordan, I want you to meet my sister. Can I pick you up tomorrow night? Bring you to my house to meet her?"

Why was he being so secretive about a sister and niece? What story could there be? "Of course."

"Thank you." His shoulders eased. A hint of a smile crossed his face for the first time. "I know you're giving me another chance after last night, and I want you to know—"

She interrupted him with her hand. "We're just talking, Cam."

"I know, but I can't imagine letting you go the way Matt did. Matt was a fool for not grabbing you up."

Was she hearing him right? Who was this—a Cam look-a-like? "I don't know what to say."

"Just give me a chance." His fingers tangled briefly with hers. "Tell your brothers to spare me. 'Cause I don't think I can hide how I feel about you anymore."

Dead ends. Every. Single. One.

He tossed his pen onto the bedspread and leaned back against the headboard. Outside his hotel window, Sunday marched into Monday. Even the nearby highway seemed to be quieting.

He was never going to figure this out if he didn't sleep.

He closed the laptop and set it, his yellow notepad, and pen on the table by the window. Peterson, his client, said there was no way he'd identified the wrong guy. This Cameron Winters had a friend who'd been caught up in a love triangle gone wrong, a huge media story about the baseball player that had been all over the news a year ago. That's where Peterson had seen Winters—on TV coverage, with his friend and the friend's girlfriend heading into a courthouse to testify. It had taken some doing to ID this nameless friend who wasn't a part of that media blitz, but Thomas had done it. And Peterson swore that Cameron Winters was Hannah Rice's—or Hannah Winters' or whatever she went by now—brother. Peterson had met him once, just before it had all started. And Peterson never forgot a face.

Hopefully Peterson was right.

In the bathroom, Thomas stared at his bleary eyes in the mirror. He had a few more places online where he could look for Hannah. And if that didn't pan out…

He took out one contact, then another. He didn't want

to tip his hand yet, but if Hannah didn't show up, he'd just have to find out what Winters' neighbors knew.

And if they didn't know anything...

Then maybe Hannah really had disappeared off the face of the earth.

CHAPTER FIVE

Cam had offered to pick Jordan up after he got off work Monday afternoon, but Jordan declined, not knowing exactly what the evening would hold. She'd meet his sister, yes, but everything else seemed so vague. So secretive, when she couldn't imagine any terrible secrets a sister might hold. Right now being able to leave at any time was an option worth having.

Jordan parked in Cam's driveway, next to his Altima, and he opened his front door as she stepped out of the car. "Hey, there," she said, smiling up at him, pretending and hoping that everything was fine.

"Hey." He met her at the bottom of his front steps. "Thanks for coming."

It was tempting to reach out and touch him, but she kept her hands to herself. "No problem. I'm just curious to hear what this big secret is."

His gaze was serious. "I'm glad I finally get to tell someone." He gestured toward the front door. "You ready to go in?"

She followed him, scanning the neighborhood with its

signs of summer about to burst. Birds chirped in a neighbor's tree, and warm sunlight cast shadows across front yards. A few cars parked on the street, and farther down the road a handful of kids on bikes chased each other.

Everything looked normal. Seemed normal. What she would hear might change all that.

Cam held the door for her. "After you."

Inside, the sounds of someone working came from the kitchen.

"Have you eaten?" he asked.

"No, actually. Is your sister making something?"

"Yeah. If it's okay with you, we'll get her kids eating in the kitchen and take our food in the dining room so we can talk."

Whatever he needed.

Cam led her into the kitchen where a woman in her mid-thirties with medium brown hair the same color as Cam's stirred something in a pot on the stove. She turned as they entered, her attention locking onto Jordan. Her smile wasn't strong, but it wasn't scared either. The woman dried her hands on a dish towel. "You must be Jordan. I'm Anna."

Jordan took the hand Anna offered. "It's nice to meet you, Anna."

The woman's features relaxed. "I've heard a lot about you. It's great to finally meet you, after all this time."

And yet she'd heard nothing about this sister, about any of his family, really.

"Need any help?" Cam asked Anna.

"Just call the kids, if you don't mind."

He headed for the sliding doors off the family room.

So there were more children than just Sophie. And, somewhere, there had to be a father. Maybe he was at their home? His and Anna's? "Do you live nearby, Anna?"

She hesitated. "I'm actually living here with Cameron right now."

Why did his sister live with him? Where was the father? Jordan pressed her lips together.

Anna must have read her curiosity. "Jordan, I promise there's a reason for everything, and we'll explain it all. I don't think there's anything Cameron wants to keep from you."

"I'm glad to hear it."

"Me too." Anna filled plates with salad and what looked like arroz con pollo from the pot on the stove.

The fragrant smell of the flavored chicken and rice woke Jordan's taste buds.

"It's been a very long time since he's talked about a woman the way he talks about you." Anna sent Jordan a grateful smile. "He's been the best brother I could ever have, and it makes me happy to think that he's found you."

Either Cam was far more confident in their relationship than Jordan realized or Anna was spilling more than he'd be comfortable with. "Cam's always been so quiet about his life, almost like he didn't have one before a few years ago. I don't know what to make of this."

The sliding glass door in the family room beyond the kitchen cut the conversation short. Two elementary-aged kids, a boy and girl about ten and eight, ran in. Both seemed to have the same hair and coloring as Anna.

Cam followed and closed the door behind them.

Neither child was the girl from the picture.

Where was this Sophie?

The kids were almost to the kitchen island before either noticed Jordan. They both pulled up short and stared at her.

The boy, the older of the two, pushed a pair of glasses higher onto his nose. "Who's this?"

Jordan fought a smile.

"Logan," Anna said, her voice hinting her displeasure at his lack of manners. "This is Jordan, a friend of Uncle Cameron's."

Logan's serious expression vanished, and a smile lit his features. "Hi," he said with a small wave.

"I'm Avery," his younger sister said. "Are you Uncle Cam's girlfriend?"

Behind them, Cam narrowed his eyes a bit and sent Jordan a faint smile. "She's a good friend. Don't you two scare her off."

Logan gaped over his shoulder at his uncle, his expression showing how funny he found it that his uncle might have a girlfriend. Any second now, the kid would probably break into that chant about the two of them in a tree.

Jordan couldn't resist. "I need you two to tell me every good story you've got on him so I'll know if I should stick around or not."

Instead of the laughter and teasing she expected, both kids gave her serious expressions. "Uncle Cam's the best," Avery said. "And he needs someone to marry and take care of him. Just like you do, Mommy."

Anna's smile was sad. "Why don't you two sit at the island and eat your dinner? We adults are going to eat in the dining room."

Jordan swallowed the lump in her throat. She'd expected joking, teasing, something lighthearted. But the sadness and seriousness of Avery's words… She was just a child. Why would she react like that?

What had this family gone through?

Cam's fingertips nudged the small of Jordan's back as Anna carried the main dish into the dining room on the other side of the kitchen wall.

Dinner started out normally enough. They made small talk while they ate, Anna asking questions about Jordan's college experience, how her job search was going, about her family and growing up in the Chicago suburbs.

"What about you?" Jordan asked when her plate was almost empty. "Where did you guys grow up?"

Anna pushed back her plate and folded her arms on the table. "Kentucky. Our parents raised horses, raced them, did really well. Still do, we hear."

She *heard?* Jordan glanced across the table at Cam.

His elbow rested on the table, a hand cupped over his mouth. He stared vacantly at the tabletop.

Evidently the story had begun.

Anna linked her hands together and studied them. "My husband was a Marine. He was stationed at Camp Pendleton in California when…" She circled her hand in the air. "When all of this began.

"I worked at a hair salon in the area and had some pretty wealthy civilian clients. One of them, Joelle Peterson, and I became good friends. Her husband was an infertility doctor, and ironically they'd been trying forever to have kids, but it just wasn't working. I knew how badly she wanted a child, and I really thought she'd be a great mom. I was a fairly new Christian—"

"Which was not how we were raised," Cam interrupted.

"Right. We weren't, and Joelle and I would talk about God, about having kids, raising a family. Anyway, Avery was just a baby at the time. Joelle had been my client throughout the entire pregnancy, and she knew how easy pregnancy had been for me. One day she came in and started talking about how she and her husband were looking into surrogacy so they could have a child of their own. And as we talked, I just felt like I should do it for her. I should be her surrogate."

A surrogate mother? Jordan clenched her fingers together on her lap. What a decision.

"So I volunteered. And come to find out, that's exactly what she'd hoped I would do. I'd had two easy, no-complication pregnancies back to back. Two healthy babies. Easy labor and delivery. Plus being a surrogate would almost double our income for the year. And she was a friend I felt deserved to be a mom." Anna met Jordan's eyes. "Why wouldn't I volunteer to help her have a baby?"

"Did you do it?"

"I did. I met her husband. They met my husband. We had long talks about it, about the procedures, the medication, the timing. Tony, my husband, needed some convincing, but the money finally did it." She smiled. "We started the process." Her smiled faded. "The first embryos didn't take. Joelle was heartbroken of course. But we tried again, and lo and behold, it worked. I was pregnant with their baby."

Cam shot her a smile. "Which was the craziest thing."

Anna laughed. "It was. You visited me right after we found out the embryo took, and you were pretty weirded out by it."

"Definitely. Even Mom and Dad were. They thought you were insane to go through with it."

"Yeah." Sadness colored Anna's single word.

And then colored Cam's face.

So there was more to the story.

"I was four months pregnant when Tony—" Anna faced Jordan, set her shoulders, and firmed her lips. "Tony was killed in a training exercise. An accident."

Oh, how awful. Jordan's hand flew to her lips. "I'm so sorry."

"Thank you." Anna swallowed. "It's been over five years now, but…"

Jordan glanced at Cam. How awful to lose a husband. To be alone and responsible for children like that.

"I had to go on, though, you know? My parents, of course, came out for the funeral, and I started the process of moving on with my life. I decided to stay there in California because of the pregnancy. Then the Petersons wanted to do some testing on the baby, right about halfway through, just to make sure everything was okay. I didn't think anything of it." Anna paused.

Jordan almost couldn't stand the suspense. "And?"

"Sophie had Down Syndrome."

Sophie was the child? The Petersons' child?

"They wanted to abort and try again."

Oh no. "Obviously they changed their minds."

Anna glanced at Cam, who sighed and pushed himself against his chair back.

He shook his head. "Jordan, they didn't change their minds."

All of a sudden so much fell into place. The secrecy, never talking about his family, never talking about the past. "What happened? Did you run?"

"Eventually. I fought it as long as I could. I was a firm believer—still am—that every life is a gift from God, that it's his decision to decide when life ends. Not ours. But California law didn't give me a voice because I wasn't the actual mother. The law there says that before the child is born, the intended mother—Joelle—is the natural and legal parent. Same with her husband. I had no say."

Cam cleared his throat. "The husband was really the one who wanted the abortion. He convinced his wife that they could do this again. They'd either pay Joelle more for another go at it or find another surrogate. He didn't care. He wanted a child, yes, but he wanted a perfect child. He felt they both deserved a 'perfect' child."

Jordan shook her head, heart breaking for where this story had to be heading. "That's terrible."

"It was. Here I am, still reeling from the loss of my husband, dealing with my two children who are mourning their dad, all while I'm now visibly pregnant with a child the parents want to kill. And while Sophie wasn't my child, she was the last big decision Tony and I made together. I refused to let them do it.

"So, yes, finally I ran. I'd been talking to a lawyer, working through my options since the contract I'd signed didn't specifically mention abortion. Just medical tests and procedures. The only option I had was to give birth in a state that would recognize me as the mother instead of the Petersons as parents."

There were states that would do that? "But you weren't the mother."

Anna laughed. "I know. It's crazy, isn't it? Michigan is one of those states that doesn't recognize surrogacy contracts. There, whoever gives birth is the legal mother. So that's where I went."

"And they let you go?"

Cam and Anna eyed each other.

"We're not sure if they let her go or just couldn't find her in time," Cam finally said.

"The nurse who always assisted Dr. Peterson when I was in his office called me—"

"Wait, the guy whose kid you were having did the procedure? Is that legal?"

Anna shrugged. "It was what he did for a living, and he was one of the best. I always assumed it made perfect sense for him to do it. He didn't have to worry about expenses and such because it was his practice, his time."

Interesting.

"Anyway, the nurse called me, left a message on my phone, and asked if we could meet. And then she was killed in a car accident the next day."

Shivers crawled down Jordan's spine.

"I thought it was more than a coincidence that this nurse wanted to talk to me when the Petersons and their lawyer were pressuring me to have an abortion. It scared me. I packed up overnight and left."

Jordan leaned back in her seat, letting the details sink in. Anna was pretty tough to fight for an unwanted child when her whole world was dangerously close to imploding.

"The Petersons knew already, though, that I was not only determined to give birth to Sophie but then raise her myself. I wasn't going to give her life and abandon her, you know? So while I don't think they ever found me in Michigan, I also don't know that they didn't just say, 'Fine. Let her have the baby and raise her.' I just don't know."

"Wow." It was quite a story. "Then Sophie was born and did have Down Syndrome?"

"She did. She's just been an angel, though—" Anna seemed to choke on her words.

Cam laid his hand over Anna's, squeezed it once. "Sophie has leukemia now. She needs a bone marrow transplant."

Jordan closed her eyes. "I am so, so sorry. How's she doing?"

Cam shook his head. "She needs that transplant soon. We're still looking for the right match."

"How hard is it to match?"

Anna seemed to stuff her emotions away and straightened in her chair. "In Sophie's case, it seems like it's very difficult. I've been tested, Cam's been tested—although we haven't heard results yet—but a best match tends to come from full-blooded brothers or sisters, because they have the same parents, which leads to a better chance of having the right match. Sophie doesn't have any brothers and sisters."

"That we know of, at least."

Anna pressed her lips together, her gaze on the table.

So they needed some stranger to come through. "Have you contacted the Petersons?" Jordan asked. "To see if they'd get tested?"

Cam lifted his chin. "Absolutely not—"

Anna's voice was quiet. "Yes."

Cam's mouth fell open, and Jordan knew that everything in Anna's and Sophie's—and Cam's—world had just shifted.

CHAPTER SIX

Cam stared at his sister, unable to form thoughts, aware only of how fast his heart pounded.

How dangerously, dangerously fast.

He swallowed. "Anna, you didn't."

Her eyes were damp. "Cameron, I had to. Right now they're her best chance."

He moaned and covered his face with his hands. How could she have done that? She might have just thrown her whole future away.

What about him? Didn't this put him in trouble too? How could she have done it without asking first? Or giving him a heads-up? Something?

Across the table, Jordan spoke. "I don't understand. Why is this bad?"

He'd forgotten Jordan was even there. What would she think of Anna's fears and suspicions? How scared would Jordan be to get close to him? He couldn't stand it if she pulled away, not after he'd gotten a taste of losing her Saturday night.

He blew out a deep, slow breath. "While we don't think

they've found Anna, we do know that they've contacted her in-laws at least once since Sophie was born." Cam shot Anna a glance.

She wouldn't look at him.

Of course not. Maybe his reaction had made her realize what a stupid, stupid move she'd made. Anger colored his voice. "Did they both get tested?"

"Just Joelle. She isn't even going to tell her husband. Not unless we have to."

He sighed. That was a massive relief, but still… She should have asked him first. They could have waited a little longer. Maybe. "You want me to tell Jordan the rest?"

She nodded. Her voice was low. "I'll check on the kids."

Jordan watched her go, then faced him, questions clear on her face.

"Anna's not her real name."

"I'm sorry, what?"

"Her name is Hannah. And she was really freaked out by what happened to that nurse. The message she got from her wasn't just an I-want-to-talk-to-you message. She said she had some information Anna needed to know before she made a decision about the abortion. Like she knew something that Anna didn't." How well he remembered Anna's frantic phone call, how hysterical she'd been that something would happen to her too. Or to her kids.

A shiver skittered over Jordan's shoulders. "What do you think she knew?"

"No idea, but Anna was scared out of her mind after the woman died. On top of that Anna worried they had a way of forcibly taking her to an abortion, a court order or something. Then our parents—" The betrayal had been intense. Even now, half a decade later, he sometimes still couldn't believe it. He cleared his throat and whacked his thumb against the table's edge.

"Your parents what?"

He looked toward the living room, everything in him wanting to break down and let the emotions escape. His voice came out weaker than he'd expected. "This is still so hard."

Her fingertips grazed the back of his hand.

Without thinking he linked his fingers with hers—clung to them—and met her gaze.

Concern marred her forehead, giving her those same worry lines Dillan sometimes wore.

Although a lot less often since he'd gotten together with his girlfriend. Fiancée.

What would it be like to know Jordan was always on his side? Would that make all of this easier to bear? He forced a smile. "If you marry me, you'll never have to deal with in-laws."

Breath whooshed from her. "Your parents were killed too?"

Not hardly. "They disowned us. Both of us."

Jordan's eyebrows rose. Her mouth opened as if she wanted to speak, but nothing came out.

He completely understood that response. "My parents are pretty big in the pro-choice movement. They speak up for it, financially support it, do whatever they can to promote it. And now here's their daughter caught up in a situation that's starting to get media coverage. They said it was bad publicity for their careers, for them and their beliefs." He could hear the anger in his voice, but what was the point in hiding it? In pretending he was over it?

Would he *ever* get over it?

"They wanted her to get an abortion—demanded she do what the Petersons asked. And when she said no, they cut her off. Here's their only daughter on the run, trying to take care of a child who has no say in any of this, and they completely abandon her. She was a military wife, for—" He clamped down on his tongue, old habits trying to resurface. "Yes, she received Tony's benefits after his death, but she needed help. Financial help. Which they could have given her again and again and again. And they refused."

Jordan squeezed his hand.

He shook his head, his grip on her fingers tightening. "They just threw her away. Told me not to help her either. And when I said no, my dad fired me from the family business—effective immediately, no severance, no reference, nothing—and told me not to contact them."

"Cam." She sounded breathless. Shocked. "I am so sorry."

Well, he wasn't sorry. He let go of her hand and rubbed his jaw until it hurt. He was angry. Still livid over it. What kind of people—

He blew out a deep breath. Every time he thought he'd dealt with the anger and forgiven them, it rose up from deep within, choking him in its intensity. He closed his eyes and pinched the bridge of his nose. "I shouldn't get so angry."

"How can you not? I can't imagine parents who would put anything above their own kids."

Yet that was his world. And it had marred him, scarred him. Probably more than he wanted to admit.

He shifted in his chair, took a deep breath, and pushed the anger away. For now. "Anna was sure that the Petersons were going to keep coming after her, so she legally changed her name. Dropped the *h*s in her first name and changed her last name to Jones so she'd be harder to find. She's done everything she can to limit her trail—used Tony's death benefits for a little house up near the state line and has been working at small-town hair salons, when she could be working in any high-end salon downtown."

"Why is she living here, then?"

"Because she's had to quit working since Sophie's leukemia got so bad. And Sophie's hospital is much closer to my house. It just made sense for them to move in here so she can take care of Sophie *and* Logan and Avery. Now that school's out, they pretty much spend their days at the hospital with Sophie."

"Wow. What a mom."

The best. "She's given up so much to protect one little girl. I don't think there's anyone I admire more than her."

"Totally understandable."

Cam held her gaze. Her eyes were warm and brown, caring, understanding. There was no horror in them, no body language that said she was about to hightail it out of there. Instead, she was leaning towards him, her hand still nearby as if an unspoken signal that she was there for him to hold onto if he wanted.

And how he wanted to hold onto her. To have someone steady and calm and reliable. Someone who loved him with a love that would never change.

The thoughts overwhelmed him, and again he couldn't do anything but watch her. All of his feelings for her had to be there for her to see.

In the kitchen, Anna's cell phone rang.

Cam listen as she answered it but couldn't make out her words. Maybe it was the hospital. Or Sophie's doctor. He tried not to think about what that could mean. "Jordan, there's more you need to know."

She sagged, her tone joking. "Please stop. I don't think I can take it."

He chuckled. "It's not so bad. I think." But he fiddled with his knife before speaking. "I help Anna get by."

"In what way?"

"I mean… Money's always been tight for her. She doesn't make a lot, and she's a single mom with three kids. I've been helping her out financially from the beginning."

Jordan nodded, as if it only made sense.

"She's been renting her house out since they moved here, but that's the only income she has right now. So I'm providing for them. I just thought you should know that, in case things with us…" He held out his hand, letting it convey the words he wasn't brave enough to voice.

"Are things pretty tight for you?"

"I'm okay. I make a pretty nice living right now, and even though my parents cut me off, I'd already received a good bit of money from them. Money they couldn't take back."

Her eyebrows rose, and humor danced across her lips. "Were you a trust fund baby or something?"

She had no idea the money he and Anna had come from, the fame in the horse-racing and breeding circles. "Kind of. I've used that to help Anna and the kids. There's not much left, but I'm committed to helping her as long as she needs it. She won't go without—not while I'm around."

She snagged his hand again. "I wouldn't expect you to."

She was so beautiful. So perfect. He swallowed and forced a smile. "Good."

In the kitchen, Anna's voice rose a bit.

Cam pulled his gaze from Jordan's and listened. Who was she talking to?

Jordan glanced toward the kitchen, then back at him. "Is everything okay?"

"I hope so."

"Is there anything you guys can do to resolve this? So she doesn't have to worry about the Petersons?"

How many times had he and his sister talked about that? "I'd like her to be more proactive, but she's pretty confident the law puts her in the wrong. She left a state where the child already belonged to someone else. Now another state says no, she's the mother. She's afraid that if the law got involved, she'd lose custody while it's sorted out. And she won't let that happen. Sophie's her daughter."

His precious niece, even if there was no blood relation.

In the kitchen, Anna's voice grew louder.

Cam pushed his chair back. "Why don't we go outside until she's done?"

In the front yard, the early June evening couldn't get more beautiful. The breeze was balmy and soothed as it swept over him. The sky was still light and bright, and kids played at the end of the cul-de-sac. In the yard next door, his neighbor Candace talked with another woman, while the newly-married couple two doors down jogged past.

He seated himself on the top step of his stairs, and Jordan joined him, her shoulder brushing his arm.

She tucked her knees in close and wrapped her arms around them while she scanned the neighborhood.

What would it be like to have her living here? To have this be *her* home too? "So." He balanced his arms across his knees. "What are you thinking about after all this?"

She didn't respond right away, instead pursing her lips and tilting her head as she studied the house across the street.

It was a lot to take in, and she probably hadn't even begun to think through all the ramifications. He probably hadn't either.

"I guess I wonder why you kept this such a secret. Why haven't you told anyone? Like Dillan? Someone?"

"Anna didn't want me to. She felt that the fewer people who knew, the better the odds were that they'd be safe."

"Now that I know, does that change anything? Will you tell anyone else?"

"Well…" He rubbed his hands together. "If we keep dating, I guess your family would need to know. Eventually."

"If we *keep* dating?" Jordan bumped his shoulder, that smile of hers creating one of his own. "You're being kind of presumptuous here, Winters. Are we dating?"

He felt himself flush a little and shoved down fears of her walking away. Jordan wasn't like that. "After tonight it doesn't make sense for me to hide how I feel." He prayed he looked calm. "I really want to date you, Jordan. I don't need you to make a commitment or anything if you're not ready, but I know… I know I don't want to date anyone but you."

She bit her lip, but a grin escaped anyway.

She was so bad at concealing her feelings. He couldn't contain his laugh. "You're happy about that?"

"Yes. Definitely. Have you talked to Dillan about us? Or Garrett?"

Definitely was his new favorite word. "I haven't. But I will. Right away, if you want."

"Do any of the other girls you've dated know about Anna?"

He'd been stupid to waste time on other women. "Not one."

"None of them?"

"None of them. Anna's the one who told me it was time to tell you. Seriously, Jordan, she's heard a lot about you. For a while now."

"I'm flattered."

She did look happy about it. Cam lost himself in her gaze. Why hadn't he taken her out to the backyard where they could have had some privacy? Where he could maybe have kissed her—

"Cam?" someone called.

Candace, his neighbor, crossed their adjoining driveways, her conversation with the other neighbor over.

"Hey, Candace." He flashed the older woman a smile. "How are you?"

"I'm fine. Just fine. Who's your friend?"

"This is Jordan, my..." His what? He leaned in to her. "How do I introduce you? Are we official?"

She scrunched her shoulders together, her grin contagious. "Let's be official."

He linked his hand with hers. "Candace, this is my girlfriend, Jordan. Jordan, my neighbor, Candace."

"Well, well, well. Cam Winters with a girl." Candace winked at Jordan. "We were all beginning to think he'd be a confirmed bachelor."

Jordan dramatically flipped her hair over her shoulder. "He was just waiting for me."

"Well, I wish you two the best. I'm sorry to interrupt, but were you home when that man went through the neighborhood?"

"What man?"

"There was a guy who came by around noon. Janet said he knocked on her door too. His niece had gotten lost in the neighborhood, and he and her dad were looking for her. I guess she's got Down Syndrome, just like your niece."

Jordan sucked in a breath, reminding Cam to take one himself. Every good feeling was as gone as if it had never been. "What'd you tell him?"

"I told him I hadn't, except for little Sophie of course. How's she doing these days?"

Oh this couldn't be good. Not after what Anna had done, calling Sophie's bio parents. "She could be better," he answered, mouth tight. His whole body tensed. "This guy—what'd he look like?"

Candace shrugged. "Mid-forties, dark hair—although it

was thinning a bit. Seemed friendly enough. Why? Is something wrong?"

Yes, everything. Was this just a coincidence? Or did it mean Anna would have to run again? Change her name again?

Only she couldn't. Not this time. Not with Sophie in the hospital.

Jordan's shoulder bumped his as she leaned toward Candace, and only then did he realize Jordan had answered for him. And he'd missed it.

But whatever she'd said seemed to satisfy Candace. "We're all hoping she gets that transplant soon," Candace said. "She's such a little sweetheart. Well, I'll leave you two lovebirds alone. Jordan, very nice to meet you."

"You too, Candace."

His neighbor wasn't even off his driveway before Cam was on his feet. "We need to tell Anna." He stood on the top step and scanned the street. All the faces he recognized. The cars—no, there were two he didn't know. Both looked empty, but could one of them belong to this man looking for a little girl with Down Syndrome? Looking for his Sophie?

How had this perfect evening gone downhill so fast?

God, why can't Anna just live her life? Cam was sick to death of her always looking over her shoulder. Could she stand to face all those fears again?

Anger rose up, taunting him at how far he still had to go in forgiving all the wrongs done to him. To his sister. To Sophie.

In the kitchen, Anna was just ending her phone call. She

faced Cam and Jordan, her face pale.

Wait until she heard the latest. "My neighbor said some guy came by today, looking for a girl with Down Syndrome."

He expected her to seem shocked by the news—to gasp or react in fear. Instead, she leaned against the island, her hand over her forehead as if she were weary.

"Did you *know?*" How could she? She'd been at the hospital all day.

"Cameron." She sent him a look that begged him to... to what? Understand? "Joelle just called."

Joelle Peterson? Cam swallowed. Why had Anna ever agreed to be a surrogate? Why hadn't God stopped her from getting tangled up in this mess?

"I'll let you guys talk."

Cam reached for Jordan.

At the same time, Anna spoke. "No. I'd like you to hear this, Jordan. If it's okay, Cameron."

He gripped Jordan's hand and nodded for his sister to continue.

"Joelle just found out she's not a match for Sophie. At all."

What? Cam squinted at his sister. He couldn't have heard that right. That didn't make any sense. "That's got to be a mistake."

"I know, but Joelle's sure. She's not a match."

"But she's her biological mother—"

No.

No, Joelle wasn't.

Not if she wasn't a partial match.

"This means you'll have to keep looking for a match for Sophie, right?" Jordan asked. "Do you think Joelle's husband has been tested?"

"Jordan." Cam faced her, hating the path his words were going to take him, Anna, and Sophie down. If only the night had ended with the stranger in the neighborhood. But now this. "They test people for matching HLA markers. Proteins. And a biological parent is a guaranteed fifty-percent match because the child gets half her HLA genes from each parent."

Cam watched understanding register on Jordan's face. "But if she isn't even a fifty-percent match…"

Anna wrapped her arms tightly across her chest. "Then we're all wondering who really is Sophie's biological mother."

CHAPTER SEVEN

Jordan shook her head. This didn't make any sense. "How can Joelle not be the biological mother? She's sure she wasn't given wrong information? That happens."

Cam swung his gaze back to Anna, fierceness in his eyes.

But Anna shook her head. "I asked her that. Over and over. She doesn't understand it either. She's made sure. She's positive the results are right. Somehow she is *not* Sophie's bio mom."

Cam wrapped his linked hands around the back of his neck, strain radiating through his arms and chest. "Who is then?"

"Joelle wondered if I got the wrong embryos."

"How possible is that?"

"I don't know!" Anna took a desperate step in one direction, then another. "Cameron, this had to be what that nurse wanted to talk about. She *knew* Joelle wasn't the mother."

"Then whatever embryo they gave you wasn't an accident."

If Joelle wasn't the mother, she would have no say in

Anna getting an abortion. Only the birth mother would have the right to make that choice. Wasn't that what the pro-choice movement said? A woman's right to choose?

Who was that woman?

And why was someone now almost on Cam's doorstep, looking for a little girl with Downs?

Jordan laid a hand on Cam's arm. "What about the man Candace mentioned?"

"What man?" Anna asked.

Of course Cam's earlier words hadn't registered, not with the news Anna had been processing. "Cam's neighbor said a man knocked on her door today, looking for a lost little girl with Down Syndrome and wondering if she'd seen anyone like that in the neighborhood."

Cam's quiet voice belied the bomb he was about to drop. "Anna, Candace mentioned Sophie to him."

Anna buried her face in her hands. Her shoulders shook.

And on the other side of the island Jordan struggled with what to do. How quickly Anna's world was falling apart.

Again.

Cam went to his sister and held her in his arms, her still-covered face buried in his shoulder.

Only then did her silence give way to muffled sobs.

God, please. Help them. What can we do? Jordan wiped moisture from the corner of her eyes.

Cam ran a hand over Anna's shuddering back. "We need to get you out of here, Anna. All of you."

Anna pulled back. "I won't leave Sophie."

"That's fine, but he knows you're here. *Here.* You can't be *here* anymore. We've got to find some safe place."

Panic filled her voice. "But where?"

Jordan raised a hand. "I can take them somewhere."

Cam and Anna searched her face.

"Can we find her a hotel? Somewhere near the hospital? I can take her in my car."

Cam shook his head. "I don't want you involved."

"I *am* involved. You've told me everything that's happened."

"No—"

"All of this new stuff happened while I was here. Why is that? Because maybe you need my help."

Her words closed his mouth.

She understood his struggle. She did. And how awesome was he for wanting to protect her too.

But it was clear now that being a part of Cam's life meant being involved in this drama that affected everything they did. He couldn't keep her out of this *and* in his life.

"Okay." He nodded as if convincing himself. "Okay. We can do this. Anna, get the kids inside and start packing. Jordan and I will figure out the details."

Tears rolled down Anna's cheeks. "Cameron, I hate this."

"We all do. But until we know better what's going on, we need to move you guys. If this man was looking for Sophie, we'll run into him again." His face darkened. "I look forward to that."

The plan took little time to work out. Cam found a hotel near Sophie's hospital and booked a room for Anna and the kids. Jordan convinced him to let her pull her car into the empty side of his garage so she could hide Anna, her kids, and their belongings in her car, then take them to their hotel. Cam would watch to see if anyone followed her.

She half-hoped someone would. Then they might get a visual on who they were dealing with.

"What about Dillan?" Cam asked suddenly.

"What about him?"

"Can he meet you there? At the hotel? I don't like you four alone, without someone to protect you."

"You want me to see what he's doing? He's probably with Miska."

Cam hesitated.

"Are you ready to tell him about this?"

His eyes searched hers. "He and Miska still have their own issues with that trial they're involved in. I hate to put more on him."

"Cam, he's your friend. You're in his wedding. Let him help."

He pressed his fingertips against closed eyelids, as if the weight of so many lay on his shoulders. "I envy you all, Jordan. I envy your parents' love, the way you take care of each other..." His shoulders shook once—twice.

The motion jerked tears to her own eyes. She pulled her chair next to his and wrapped her arms around his shoulders.

How long had he been carrying this alone? And none of them had even known. "Call Dillan," she whispered. "Let him help, Cam. Please don't deal with this by yourself."

He sniffed deeply and pulled himself out of her embrace. "Sorry."

"What do you have to be sorry for? All I see is how tough you are. How strong and dependable."

He cast a heartbroken gaze her way.

"Seriously, Cam. I think I've fallen more in love with you these last few minutes than in the whole month before."

He closed the inches between them and planted a firm kiss on her lips.

Jordan closed her eyes.

He kissed her again, his lips slow and gentle this time, saying everything she'd hoped he felt about her. His hand caressed her cheek a moment before he pulled back. "Jordan." His eyes searched hers. "Can we get married?"

She laughed.

He chuckled with her. "I'm halfway not kidding."

"I know." She eased back in her seat and held his hands in hers, hoping he could see how she felt about him too. "I love hearing you say that."

"Yeah. But…"

"There's no *but*. I like that you're thinking that way."

"Good." He smiled, the heaviness gone from his eyes but his cheeks a bit pink. He sniffed again. "I'll call Dillan."

"I'll see if Anna needs any help."

Jordan headed up the stairs, past the spot where she'd seen that teddy bear and toy car two days earlier, which all made sense now.

Voices came from the first bedroom on the right.

Jordan knocked on the open door. "Need any help?"

Anna looked up from the open suitcase on the bed. Beside her, little Avery held purple pajamas and a stuffed blue beaver, her eyes somber. "I'm not sure," Anna said. "What's Cameron decided?"

Jordan entered the room and ruffled Avery's fine brown hair. "I'm going to drive you guys to the hotel."

"You are?"

"Cam's going to follow. A little later."

Anna nodded, clearly catching everything she hadn't said. "Thank you, Jordan."

"You're very welcome."

Avery watched her intently.

Jordan flashed her a smile. "Are you excited about staying in a hotel?"

Avery glanced at her mom, as if she didn't know herself.

"You're bringing your swimsuit, right? This one has a pool."

Her eyes lit up. "Can we, Mommy?"

Anna laughed. "We'll do it."

Avery flew to her dresser, pulled out the bottom drawer, and rummaged through it.

The look Anna shot her was filled with gratitude. "I was a little nervous how you'd take all of this. But look at you. Rolling with the punches."

Jordan shrugged. "You guys don't have much of a choice, do you?"

"Well, I don't." Anna sighed. "I'm really sorry how all this affects Cameron. I know that means it'll affect you too."

"Don't be sorry. You gave your little girl life. You fought for her when no one else would."

"There wasn't any other option. I knew Tony would have agreed. I had to defend her." Anna lowered her voice. "I just wish I hadn't been so naïve going into the whole thing. I never dreamed anything could make Dr. Peterson want to abort his own child."

"Or whoever's child she is."

"Right." Anna's eyes widened. "I guess he wouldn't be the father either. And here he's demanding that I get an abortion."

"It's messed up, isn't it?"

Anna glanced over her shoulder at Avery, who was closing her drawer, bright pink swimsuit in hand. "Avery, why don't you and Logan pick out some movies to take with us?"

When Avery left, Anna turned to Jordan. "He's hiding something, that's for sure. Which has got to be why someone is canvassing this street, pretending to look for a little girl."

"Joelle has no idea what that secret would be?"

"I don't think so."

"What did her husband say when she asked him whose egg he used?"

"I don't think she's confronted him yet."

Oh no. Joelle was in trouble. Or about to be. "Anna—"

Her eyes widened. "I need to warn her."

Jordan waited while Anna called, prayed the woman would answer, that she hadn't said anything to her husband yet.

But Joelle didn't answer.

Anna called again. Left a message telling her not to say

anything to anyone—if she hadn't already. And asking her, begging her, to call right back.

The silent cell phone shook in Anna's hand.

"She really was my friend, Jordan. She celebrated with me the whole time I was pregnant with Avery, even though she still couldn't have a baby. We talked about God, about family, about how hard life could be—" She covered her mouth with her hand. "I couldn't stand it if something happened to her."

"You can't worry about that, Anna. Not right now. We need to take care of you and the kids."

"And Sophie."

Yes, Sophie. "Did you contact the hospital?"

Anna nodded. "I let them know that something was going on and to be extra careful about anyone who might try to get to her. The nurses there know me. They'll take this seriously."

Good. One less thing, maybe, to worry about. "What else can I do?"

"Pray. Pray that…" Anna stared at Avery's bed, searching the covers as if for some thought or the right words. "Pray that this stops. For your sake. For Cameron's. For all of ours. Cameron's right. I can't live like this forever."

CHAPTER EIGHT

Anna and the kids were settling into the hotel room when Dillan called Jordan. "We're here," he said. "What do you want us to do?"

"Are you in the lobby?"

"Still in the car. Should we wait here?"

"That might be best. Give me a couple minutes. I'll call you back."

"Okay."

"Wait, Dillan?"

"Yeah?"

"Will you watch who comes in and out? Maybe someone who drives in and just stays in their car? Watching?"

He chuckled. "Like us?"

Jordan smiled as she hung up.

Anna looked up from tucking a suitcase into the closet. "Was that Cameron?"

"No, my brother. He's here, keeping an eye on things in the parking lot. I wonder if Cam's seen... anyone."

Anna glanced at the far bed where the kids were huddled around a tablet. "I'm not sure if I want him to or not."

"I know exactly what you mean." Her phone rang, and Cam's picture popped up. "Here's your brother." She answered. "So where are you?"

"I'm home, actually. Watching everything from my front door. Ever seen *Rear Window*? I'm feeling a bit Jimmy Stewart-ish right now."

"Does that make me Grace Kelly?"

"That sounds about right. When are you going to come over and feed me and let me admire how beautiful you are?"

Anna peeked at Jordan, a smile across her lips.

"Cam, I think your sister heard that."

"Tell her we'll behave."

Her cheeks warmed, remembering their first kiss an hour earlier. "You don't think anyone followed us?"

"I don't think so. Your idea of hiding them in your car seems to have worked. If anyone *was* watching."

That was the big question. "Now what?"

"I guess you can leave. I'll head there in a bit and see if they need anything."

Anna brushed by Jordan on her way to the bathroom. "Tell him we're fine, and he doesn't need to come."

"I heard that," he said.

"Are you still coming here?" Jordan asked.

"No. Although I'm not sure I can sit here for the rest of the evening either."

"Nothing to do?"

"No one to talk to. I'm feeling kinda lonely, Jordan."

She smiled at the playful pout in his voice. "You want to come over? We can hang out with my family. Probably get some time to talk alone too."

"I'm half-terrified and half-jazzed at the idea. Meet you there?"

Jordan grinned. "Meet you there."

Cam's car was already parked in her parents' driveway when Jordan pulled in. Dillan and Miska had left the hotel to continue their own date, and Garrett was probably at his downtown condo. She wouldn't have to share Cam with anyone—except maybe her parents.

How long had Cam been here? And what had the conversation with her parents been like? How much had he told them?

Inside, Cam sat in her living room with Mom and Dad, the three of them talking while a Cubs game played on the TV.

Cam stood when she entered, smiling her way, but Dad spoke first. "You do know, Jordan, that he's a Reds fan?"

Cam chuckled.

Jordan met his gaze. So there *had* been a conversation. "I'm willing to make sacrifices."

Dad shook his head, pretending to be appalled.

"Mom, Dad, we're going out on the deck to talk."

"Fine. But don't listen to a word he says about baseball."

Outside, the sky had faded to periwinkles and purples, magenta, and the faintest peach.

Jordan skipped the patio table—too close to the kitchen window—for the top step of the two-level deck and sat down.

Cam seated himself beside her. "That went well."

"You talked to my parents?"

"I did. I told them I was very interested in you."

It would have been nice to have witnessed that conversation herself. "Very, huh? And they said...?"

"They seemed good with it. No one called me too old or you too young. Your dad actually seemed to like the idea."

"And my mom?"

"I guess I didn't catch her reaction."

"If she didn't say anything, she's probably good with it too." Now for her brothers. "Have you talked to Dillan or Garrett?"

"I told Dillan tonight. I called him before I called you. He thinks we were slowpokes." He eyed her, clearly thinking about how to say something.

And evidently struggling with it.

She nudged him with her shoulder. "What?"

He linked his fingers together and frowned at them. "I don't want to be slow about the rest of this."

The rest of this... His meaning dawned on her. She widened her eyes and faked a shocked expression. "Are you asking me to elope?"

"No." He grinned at the vast, empty park beyond the backyard. "I'd like to have a good relationship with my future in-laws, seeing as how they may be the only parent figures I ever have."

"Did you tell them about your sister?"

"Not yet. I'm not sure if... I would have, until everything that happened tonight." He slid his hand over hers and wove their fingers together. "I don't want them thinking I'm putting you in any danger. And then I have to stop and think. Am I?" He met her gaze. "Do you think I'm putting you in danger?"

When he held her hand like this? Shared the most private part of his heart with her? "No," she whispered.

"Good."

But he let her hand go and rubbed his palms together.

Why did he go back and forth like that? Comfortable then uncomfortable in a few seconds?

Evidently there was more he needed to say. If only he'd spit it out. While it was tempting to ask him what it was, it'd be best if he told her on his terms. She shouldn't force whatever it was out of him before he was ready.

Before they were both ready.

"So we're not going to elope, we're not going to get married before Dillan and Miska do. What's the plan, then?"

"Get to know each other. Well."

"I like that plan."

"Maybe you will, maybe you won't."

What did that mean? "Why? Is your favorite color neon pink?"

He pretended surprise. "You saw my bedroom?"

She laughed. "Actually, I saw the toys on the stairs Saturday and wondered if you had some… toy issues."

"Really? You hid that well."

"You don't have a bedroom full of stuffed bears? Or Matchbox cars all over your pink dresser?"

"Umm…"

She gave him a playful shove. "Stop it."

"Avery's the one into cars, actually. Logan's outgrowing them, but she loves them. We've got a racetrack set up in the basement. The two of us spend good time down there."

What an awesome uncle he was. "Maybe she'll grow up to be a racecar driver."

Cam grimaced. "Her mom would love that."

Silence settled around them, and nature filled it. A bird chirped high in one of the trees, and across the yard another answered it. Were they a couple? A family? Were there young birds somewhere close by?

"So." Cam leaned forward, elbows on his thighs, and rubbed his palms together again. And again. He bit his lip, then finally nodded as if he'd come to some decision. "I, uh, got my girlfriend pregnant in high school."

Oh.

"My senior year. Early in the year. She, umm…"

Jordan's throat tightened.

"I already told you about my parents. How pro-choice they are. Her family wasn't. They were a lot more conservative, but of course I had my parents' viewpoint on it. Just end it, you know?"

When would he look at her? When he'd finished?

"That's what I wanted her to do, but she wasn't sure. So I had her talk to my parents. They weren't happy with me, but they felt there was an easy solution. That neither of us had to suffer."

"*Suffer?*"

She didn't realize she'd said it out loud until Cam looked her way. "That was their word. You know, we didn't need to have those consequences. We didn't have to let it 'become a child.'" He used his fingers for air quotes. "I just went with it. Thought sure, we can fix this. And I didn't listen to her. At all."

A mosquito buzzed by her ear. Jordan swatted it away, her hand feeling weak.

"It all really hit me—what I'd done to her—when Anna went through it. The pressure to abort, knowing it wasn't right. Knowing it was a real child in there. A little person." His jaw clenched as he sat silent for several seconds. "I was about the biggest jerk a guy could be. I didn't care what my girlfriend thought. I just wanted that baby gone, and I was getting angry that she was so hesitant about it. Always crying. Always…" A small groan escaped him, and he closed his eyes, a deep breath dropping his shoulders. "I pressured her. Hard. Convinced her finally. And she did it. Because I wanted it."

Oh, Cam. Her eyes fell shut, but moisture leaked from them. Tears for a lost child, for the teenage girl he'd pushed to do something she didn't want to do, for Cam himself— all these years later.

And for her own pain, right in this moment. For knowing more of what was in his past.

"Jordan." He pulled her to him, and she rested her head against his collarbone. His words were deeper than normal, his voice rougher. "I'm sorry."

She nodded against him. Deep down, she'd known there was something more. Cam had only become a Christian a handful of years ago. And his silence had made everyone wonder what kind of a life he'd come from. So while this wasn't a surprise exactly…

"I hate telling you this. I hate that I could have a teenager now. I wish I did. I wish so much that I did."

"Cam, I'm not mad." She sat up and wiped beneath her eyes. "I'm sorry for all of it too."

He watched her closely, as if he wasn't quite sure he believed her.

She forced a shaky smile for him. "I'm okay. Really."

His mouth twitched into a smile. "Thank you."

She nodded.

He pulled her close again and pressed his lips against her hair. "You're awesome," he breathed above her ear.

And so was he. Look how far he'd come from what he'd been. "What happened to her?"

He released her and spoke toward the park again. "I haven't heard anything about her in the last few years, but last I did hear… Her life's a mess."

"Guilt?"

"I think so. I realize now that she was trying all kinds of things to self-medicate. She went wild, then joined some weird religion. I heard she tried to kill herself in college. She just became a completely different person, swinging from one extreme to the other."

Looking for help. For answers.

"And then Anna gets into a similar situation and refuses to have an abortion. I didn't get it. I didn't push her to do it—I'd learned at least that much. But I watched her. Listened. Helped however I could."

"To make up for…" How did she finish that line?

"I don't think so. It just confused me why she would risk everything for a child that wasn't even hers. I mean, I understood at first. If she didn't give that child a voice, no one else would. But I really thought that once the parents refused to be convinced, she'd say okay."

"But she didn't."

He shook his head. "Just the opposite. She told me it was wrong, that the baby had been given life, and she would not end it. Would *not*. I'd argue, and we'd talk about it. About God giving life. About what the Bible said about life. Did you know that the church fathers spoke out against abortion?"

"Really?"

"Yeah. I started reading up on it, and that led to more talking about the Bible, about what the church fathers believed as compared to what I *thought* they believed—"

"Which was?"

He shook his head. "I was clueless, Jordan. Knew nothing. But I was learning. And Anna was grieving over Tony and talking about how she'd see him in heaven again. I even told her not to worry about the baby, that she'd see her in heaven too." He grimaced. "I still can't believe I said that about Sophie."

How had she not known that there was so much behind Cam? So much that had led him to where he was today? "Clearly it's not how you feel now."

"No." A soft smile covered his lips. "I became a Christian because of Sophie. Because of Anna. She fought for what she knew to be right. If she hadn't, I never would have bothered to ask why life mattered. Why Anna was about to be stuck, I thought, with someone else's disabled child. Why she was willing to lose so much for a less than perfect life. That got me searching, Jordan. *Me.* I look back and see that God used a supposedly imperfect Sophie to bring me to him. To show me how imperfect I was without him. How I needed him. How much he'd sacrificed to give *me* life. And when I got it, it just... Jordan, it blew me away."

A different kind of tear filled her eyes now. "That's amazing."

"Yeah. It is." He searched her face. "I *am* sorry that I had to tell you what I've done. I wish I could undo it all. For the sake of everyone involved. But I know God's forgiven me. I know that."

"Which is why you're helping Anna so much."

"No, I'm doing that because it's right. Letting Sophie be born was only the beginning of choosing life instead of abortion. Everything I do now is because it's what God wants me to do—to help a widow and her kids. To stand up for what's right, no matter what some law might say."

Jordan wrapped her arm around his and curled up against him, her head on his shoulder. The old Cam was hard to picture. She couldn't imagine this typically quiet, calm man doing—thinking—what he had.

How God had changed him. And how grateful she was for it.

"What's going on in your head?"

"That I'm glad you told me."

"Really?"

"Cam, I want to know you. The good, the bad. The current you, the past. I want to know why you're you."

His head rested on top of hers. "I've dreaded having to tell you this."

"I know."

"How did I get so lucky to end up with you?"

Jordan sat up and smiled at him. "Keep talking."

With a chuckle, he rested his forehead against hers, his breath warm on her face. "I really admire how you've handled this. Grace Kelly has nothing on you."

"Thank you."

His lips brushed hers once, twice, then pulled back. "I also don't think you've had time to process everything. You might not feel so understanding in the morning."

"Cam—"

"I mean it. I'm giving you room to get mad at me if you need to. To *hurt*, Jordan. I don't want you to pretend you're okay if you're not."

"I don't believe in faking emotions. In case you hadn't noticed."

"One reason I like you so much."

He pulled out of her touch and rested his palms on the deck behind him, leaning back while he watched her.

"You're not going to tell me the other reasons?"

"What other reasons?"

Tease. "Why you like me so much."

He grinned out at the park. And said nothing.

"Wow, you know how to romance a girl."

"Don't I?"

"So?"

"You do like to fish for compliments, don't you?"

"Well, you did compare me to Grace Kelly."

He fingered the ends of her hair. "I don't like blondes, though. I prefer dark hair. And eyes."

Warmth flooded through her, and she couldn't take her eyes off him. How she wanted to kiss him again, kiss him for more than a couple lingering seconds.

He released her hair and sat up. "Jordan, you and I—I want us to date right. To marry right. I've already kissed you two more times tonight than I probably should have. Because I'm having a hard time thinking past kissing you some more. A lot more."

Did she dare tell him that she was too?

"And I can tell by the look in your eyes that you're thinking the same thing."

Warmth spread across her cheeks, and she ducked her head, turned away.

"Makes me feel good, of course. A guy likes that."

She nodded. So did a girl.

"Jordan."

She wanted nothing more than to throw herself into his arms, be held by him, kissed by him. And right now she halfway felt rejected.

Was it because she knew he'd done more? With someone else?

Was this that hurt he'd mentioned, starting to surface? She closed her eyes, frustrated with the way her mood was suddenly changing.

"Jordan?" He turned her to him. "What'd I say?"

What had he said? What was this frustration building in her? "Nothing, Cam. Maybe you're right, about the hurt coming later."

His eyebrows knit in question.

Okay. Fine. "I want you to kiss me. A lot. And now

you're saying you won't. When you've…" She flipped a hand out to let it say the rest.

"Ah."

Yes. *Ah.*

"That's because I don't want to do to you what I did to her. I care about you, Jordan. I was nothing but selfish with her, but I want to protect you. And right now you might need some protecting from me. Because I know me."

His words comforted, a little. "You're right. We should just elope."

A laugh burst from him.

Jordan couldn't help smiling.

"And now I'm suspecting again that you're trying to get your brothers to kill me."

"Never."

He chuckled. "I guess we should call it a night, huh?"

"If we have to."

On his feet, he offered her his hands and pulled her up. The deck lights—when had those come on?—lit the planes of his face. His hazel eyes smiled at her.

Jordan smiled back, feeling it a bit this time. "When will I see you again?" she asked, remembering now what she was worrying about. That they'd share a special evening together and then she wouldn't hear from him for days— the way Matt had treated her for so long.

"Tomorrow night? My goal is to see if you get sick of me or not."

"It's going to take a lot more than one night to figure that out."

He winked at her. "We'll do a thorough test."

How quickly she was falling in love with this man. "Okay then. It's a date."

His gaze dipped, then flew back to her eyes. "Yes, a date."

"Nice work, Thomas."

It was, actually. Tracking Hannah down had been one of his tougher jobs in recent years. "My pleasure. I'll send you my final bill in the morning."

"Not yet. Something's come up, and I'm not going to be able to get there tomorrow. I'll need you to stay a little longer, keep an eye on things for me."

"What things?"

"Just make sure she doesn't run away, that she's still in that house, that everything's normal. That kind of thing."

"I'm happy to do it, but I'll need to charge you—"

"That's fine. Whatever it costs. All right?"

If finding Hannah had been so stinking important, why now was the guy getting cold feet about coming out to talk to her? Hadn't that been Peterson's goal the whole time? What could be keeping him from coming?

"Thomas?"

"I'll do it."

"And don't send me a bill. Just—What do I owe you? Right now? I'll send you some cash right away."

Something suddenly didn't feel right about this. "Let me figure it out and get back to you in the morning."

"Okay. Just call me with the number. Don't send a bill. Not yet."

No, things weren't right at all.

CHAPTER NINE

On Tuesday evening, Cam took Jordan to the hospital to meet Sophie, eager to show off the little girl who'd changed his life.

He'd told Jordan how loving and giving Sophie was despite everything she was going through. But in the hospital room, it was clear it had been a rough day.

Sophie slept in her bed, and Anna dozed in a nearby recliner, eyes closed until they entered, while Logan and Avery read by the window.

Anna pushed herself out of the chair and held a finger to her lips. She looked exhausted, the circles under her eyes almost matching the dark circles beneath Sophie's closed eyes.

Cam gave Anna a quick hug, then held her at arm's length to study her face. "Rough day?"

She nodded. "Worst one in a while. They gave her the wrong breakfast, then had to give her a new PICC line."

Sophie'd probably thrown a fit over it all and worn herself out. Worn Anna out too. "Sorry to hear that. How are you holding up?"

Anna flashed them a smile that said it all. That she was beyond frazzled, was close to falling apart. "I'm fine."

He hugged her tightly. "You are such a liar."

Beside him, Jordan chuckled.

Anna pushed herself back and wiped her eyes. "I'm sorry we're all such a mess, Jordan."

"It's fine, Anna. You're allowed."

She glanced over her shoulder at the sleeping girl. "I'd hoped you'd get to see her on a normal day. A good day."

"Is she asleep for the night?" Cam asked.

"No. She'll probably wake up soon."

Cam walked to Avery and Logan and ruffled Avery's hair, then tried to close Logan's book on him.

Still reading, Logan grinned and fought to keep the pages spread.

Cam let him win.

While Jordan and Anna whispered together, he crossed to Sophie's bed and squatted beside her, his arms folded on her blankets, watching her while she slept.

A soft brown knit cap, the same color as her missing hair, sat askew on her bald head. She looked so pale today. Worn out. Weary. His throat closed. *God, please. She needs a donor.*

He and Anna would hear soon if they were a match for Sophie. He hadn't been holding his breath on that one; they weren't related after all. But now… What if Anna's swab showed that fifty-percent match Sophie's mother would have? He still couldn't shake that scenario from his mind. Had Sophie been with her birth mom all this time? Did Tony have a third child he never knew about?

He searched her face, looking for similarities to his

brother-in-law, but those blue eyes of Sophie's—the ones blinking at him now—sure weren't from Tony's side of the family.

Sophie grinned at him.

Cam grinned back. "Hey, Soapy. You're awake."

She reached for him but didn't sit up, and he knew immediately how bad of a day it had been. "Unckie," she said, her voice small, her smile huge. "Unckie here."

He held her small, wide palm in his and stroked his fingers across the crease, the way she liked it. "I'm here. Couldn't go through the day without seeing my favorite girls."

She tried to sit up, and Cam rose to help her. She reached both arms for him, and he sat down next to her so she could hug him. So he could hug her.

She held him tightly and kissed his stomach.

He kissed the top of her head.

But her usual enthusiasm, her excessive greeting that warmed him every time, just wasn't there. She was too tired tonight. And weak. Way too weak. "You have a rough day, Soapy?"

She mumbled something and leaned against him, eyes closing.

This just wasn't her. His poor girl needed sleep. And a donor. Yesterday. He squinted at Anna. "She okay?" he mouthed.

Anna nodded. "Tired," she mouthed back.

"Where Dom?" Sophie asked.

"Mom's in her chair. Behind you."

Sophie looked over her shoulder, then grinned like she

hadn't seen Anna in a great while. "Dom!" She reached out one hand and waved her over with her chunky little fingers.

Anna obeyed and settled on the other side of the bed.

Somehow Sophie managed to get one arm around her mom too.

"Cameron brought a friend to meet you," Anna said.

Sophie looked up at him, her eyebrows furrowed. "Friend?"

"Her name's Jordan. Can you say that? Jordan?"

"Jor...en," she tried.

"Jordan," Cam repeated.

And then Jordan was beside him on the bed, her smile for Sophie warming him. "Hi, Sophie. I'm Jordan."

"Jordan," Sophie said again.

"That's right. I'm glad I get to meet you. Your Uncle Cam loves you lots. I can tell by everything he's told me about you."

Yeah, he loved Sophie a lot. Jordan too. He traced the dark hair around her temples, the long strands she'd made wavy today. The long, dark eyelashes around those brown eyes. It'd been so hard last night to tell her *everything*. But what a relief to know that there were no more secrets between them.

And what a relief that she was still here beside him. Still happy to be his girlfriend. To meet this little girl who'd thrown so much of his life into turmoil.

"Cam?"

Jordan was looking at him now—no, laughing at him, her smile struggling to contain itself.

And so was Anna.

Clearly he'd been caught mooning.

Oh well. As if he cared that the two women in his life knew how he felt. "Stop it. What'd I miss?"

Jordan spoke. "She asked if I'm going to take care of you like Anna takes care of her."

"Yes." Cam's nod for Sophie was emphatic. "She'll get to feed me—"

"*Get* to?"

"—and wash my laundry and pick up all my toys." He grinned at Jordan at that one. "All my Matchbox cars."

Jordan laughed and rolled her eyes.

Anna watched them. "I missed something there."

Yes, she had. "Jordan's got this weird… thing for toy cars." He shook his head sadly at Sophie. "Isn't that funny, Soapy? That someone like Jordan would play with teeny, tiny little cars?"

Sophie nodded. "I like my baby. And my bear." She suddenly searched her bed, almost frantic in the motion. "Where my bear? Where bear?"

From the bench in front of the window, Logan held up the bear, his eyes still glued to his book. His rear still glued to the window bench.

Anna took the bear—a newer version of the one Jordan had seen on the stairs—and gave it to Sophie, who was on the verge of tears.

"Bear!" She grabbed the stuffed animal and squashed it against her chest. "My bear."

A tear glistened on her eyelashes, and again Cam realized how worn out she was. She might have woken up from an early evening nap, but it sure looked like this little girl could use even more sleep. "Sophie, I think your bear needs a nap. Think you can get him to go to sleep?"

She nodded. "Bear sleep now."

"You too?"

Sophie pursed her lips. "Soapy sleep too."

Maybe she'd sleep all through the night and wake up to a much better morning. He hugged her, carefully this time, and pressed his lips to her head again. "Jordan and I will come see you later, okay? You go to sleep and get better."

"Bear get better," Sophie said. "Bear and Soapy sleep."

He straightened her cap. "Night night, Soapy."

She snuggled down beneath her blankets and held the bear's head beneath her chin. She closed her eyes and...

Was she asleep already? He studied her as he stood.

Eyes still closed, Sophie held a finger to her lips. "Be still. Bear sleeping."

There was a hint of his silly girl. He grinned at Jordan, then Anna. "Need anything before we go?"

Anna glanced at Avery and Logan, then at Jordan. "Cameron, I'm sorry—" she started.

She wanted to stay with Sophie. Of course she did. Before Jordan, it had been easy, staying home with his niece and nephew. Now... "How about we take the kids back to my place?" he asked Jordan. "You okay with a pizza for dinner?"

She threaded her fingers through his. "Sure."

"Is it safe?" Anna asked.

Right. He'd forgotten too easily. "We'll take the pizzas back to the hotel, and I'll spend the night there." He turned to Jordan. "Can I drop you and the kids off, then run home and get my stuff for tomorrow?"

"That works."

Anna whispered a thank you to her.

"Avery, Logan, ready to leave?" he called. "Get some dinner?"

The kids were off the bench immediately.

Jordan laughed at their reaction.

And Cam lost himself in her again. In the sweet, giving nature of this gorgeous woman he was falling deeply in love with.

Logan and Avery clearly couldn't be happier to be out of that hospital.

Jordan had barely unlocked the door of the hotel room before Logan was inside and running for the TV by the beds. Even Avery kicked off her shoes by the door and dashed after her brother.

Cam returned quickly with his things, ordered a pizza, and joined Jordan on the couch in the sitting area of the room. The closet and bathroom served as a bit of a divider between the living area and the sleeping quarters, giving them some privacy from his niece and nephew. Cam left some space between them, but faced her, his arm draped across the top of the couch.

When he said nothing, just sat there and smiled at her, Jordan quirked an eyebrow. "What?"

"I'm enjoying this. Being with you. Even if we're not completely alone."

Something slid and rattled back by the beds. "What are they doing?"

"I think they're setting up Life, their latest favorite game. If they ask you to play, say no."

"Why?"

He leaned closer. "Because I don't want to share you."

Her cheeks warmed, and she searched for something to say. "You didn't tell me you called Sophie 'Soapy.'"

"Avery gets credit for that. She was two, I think, when Sophie was born. And then Sophie just started using it for herself. It's pretty cute, isn't it?"

"It's adorable."

"Yeah." He sobered. "She wasn't doing very well tonight."

"She's usually better?"

"Lots. I'm hoping she's just tired and not..." He ran a hand through his hair. There was a place he wouldn't let himself go. "Her immune system is basically shot. Plus, because of the Down's, she has a hard time verbalizing where her pain is. I'm hoping she's not coming down with an infection or something."

"I'll pray she's just tired."

"Jordan?" came Avery's voice.

"Say no," Cam whispered, his lips hardly moving.

Jordan twisted in her seat.

The girl's light brown hair fell across her face, and even though she had to be happy to be out of that hospital room, sadness still lingered on her features.

"Yes, Avery?" Jordan asked.

"Do you and Uncle Cam want to watch a movie with us?"

A movie? "What happened to your board game?"

A soft growl of disapproval came from Cam.

Avery shrugged. "We changed our minds. You want to watch *Despicable Me*?"

What a fitting movie choice for this poor little family, torn apart by death—and now deception. While Anna was doing everything she could to parent her kids, there was no way the older two didn't slip through the cracks sometimes. Right now Avery looked like she needed some love.

Jordan looked Cam's way.

His head was shaking, just barely. Just enough for her to notice.

"After our pizza?" she asked him.

His eyes widened.

"Cam," she whispered and looked back at Avery, then him again.

This time he really looked at his niece—and she saw the moment he realized how much this little girl was hurting too.

"Can we wait until after we eat?" he asked her.

Avery's face brightened, and she nodded, her hair shaking across her face again.

"Okay. You guys find something to do until then."

Avery ran back to tell Logan.

Cam groaned. "Am I ever going to get some time alone with you?"

"She needs love too, Cam. Did you see how heartbroken she looked when she came in here? She looked lost."

"Yeah. She did." He sighed. "Don't tell Anna. She'll feel bad."

"You don't think she should know?"

"What can she do about it? I'm just glad she's quit working until Sophie…"

"Gets better."

His jaw tightened. "Right."

Which meant he was providing so much for them. Jordan laid her arm across the sofa back, her hand on top of his. "Does she look at you as her dad?"

"I don't think so. I don't do any disciplining or anything like that. I mean, they've only lived with me for the last six months, since Sophie's been so sick. I was always just the fun uncle before." A dry laugh escaped him. "I don't feel much like the fun uncle these days."

"Maybe they don't need a fun uncle right now. I say we watch the movie out here, squeezed into the same four-foot space on the couch, and give them lots of love."

Cam raised an eyebrow. "I'm game for that."

Cam, clearly not born and raised in Chicago, had ordered some national chain pizza. Jordan ate it anyway, sitting beside Logan and trying to outdo his knock-knock jokes during dinner. Avery made up her own jokes—which were bad enough to be funny—and dinner ended up being nothing but average pizza and lots of laughter.

When the kids had washed their hands and faces, then showered, because it was getting to be that time of night, the four of them curled up on the couch. Cam settled next to Jordan with one arm around her and the other on Logan's shoulder. Avery climbed onto Jordan's lap, and Jordan snuggled her close, her damp hair smelling of strawberries and clean skin.

Partway into the movie, Avery fell asleep, but Logan kept quoting favorite lines half a second before the movie did.

Cam sent Jordan a faint side smile, then tried to pull her even closer. "Four feet," he whispered. "Remember?"

"Fine," she whispered back, pretending annoyance even as she snuggled into his side.

His fingers slid through her hair, and his warmth surrounded her even more. He felt solid beside her. Solid, stable, and, yes, super attractive. She gave in pretending to be interested in the movie and rested her head on his shoulder, loving the feel of his chest moving beneath her.

Cam ran his hand down her hair.

Would this be them in a few years? In his home—her home?—with kids of their own?

What would that mean for Anna and her children? Would coming into Cam's life push the kids and Anna out of his? Did he have that much of himself to go around?

Avery twitched, and Cam looked down at her. "Why don't we put her in bed?"

Jordan nodded.

Cam whispered to Logan that they'd be back, then stood and scooped Avery out of her arms.

Jordan followed him and pulled down her covers. She stepped back while Cam laid Avery down and tucked her in, pausing to brush her hair away from her face before standing up.

He set his arm casually across her shoulders, his gaze still on his niece. "I could see us doing this," he finally whispered.

Jordan turned into him, her arm around his waist. "Me too."

He didn't look at her. Only nodded.

She rested her head against his shoulder. "How tall are you, Cam?"

"Where did that question come from?"

"I was planning on shoe shopping tomorrow. I need to know if I should buy heels or not."

"Like you aren't tall enough with your Foster DNA."

"This is where you're supposed to tell me that you like tall women."

"Tall women with dark hair and dark eyes." He peeked at her. "Who are also ten years younger."

"Nine years—"

He silenced her with a kiss. A quick kiss that ended too fast. He swallowed and stepped back. "I have *got* to stop doing that."

Those weren't her thoughts, exactly, but clearly he meant it. She stepped back a bit so he'd be less tempted. All of which was exactly the opposite of what she wanted.

"Jordan. I just realized you don't have a car here."

She shrugged. So far every time he'd kissed her, he'd immediately decided it was time for them to say goodnight. Maybe kissing him wasn't the best idea right now. "We'll figure it out. What about the kids in the morning? When do you have to go to work?"

"Anna will come here early. Get cleaned up and take them back with her."

And they'd spend another day in the hospital? How much time had they spent there already?

Suddenly shoe shopping didn't seem all that important. "What if I came here and stayed with them?"

He squinted at her. "What do you mean? Like all day?"

"Sure. I don't have a job yet. I've got no plans for tomorrow that can't wait—"

Cam grabbed her and hugged her close.

Didn't let go.

Jordan wrapped her arms around his back and rested there in his arms, feeling him swallow, listening to his deep breathing, enjoying the way his hand tangled in her hair.

When he finally relaxed his hold, his eyes looked suspiciously moist. "Thank you," he whispered, his voice cracking a bit. "You know you don't have to."

"I know. But I want to. They're your family. So I want to help them—help *you*—however I can."

He kissed her again, slowly, deeply this time.

Jordan wound her hands around his neck, her fingertips in his hair, lost in the tenderness that was Cam Winters.

When he pulled back—and Jordan swayed a bit on her feet—he stayed close and gazed into her eyes. "Why did I wait so long?"

"For what?"

"To be honest about how I felt about you. To think that we could have had more time together—"

"Well, we're together now. So quit sending me home every time you kiss me, and let's enjoy the rest of our evening."

He gave her one last kiss. "Deal."

CHAPTER TEN

Wednesday morning Cam greeted Jordan at the hotel room door with a kiss. "Since I'm leaving in a sec," he teased before letting her inside.

She swatted his arm. "Where are the kids?"

"Still sleeping. They may sleep all morning, and I say let them. They're probably catching up."

"Sure."

He looked good, dressed in a pale blue dress shirt and gray pants.

"You dress up for work."

"Goes with the job. The VP of marketing can't come in looking casual."

"You're the VP of marketing? Since when?"

Surprise flashed across his face. "For over a year. You didn't know that?"

"A year ago you were just Dillan's friend."

"Well, don't be too impressed. There's a VP for everything at work. On the other hand…" He surveyed her a moment, a smile creeping across his face. "It really *is* my charm she's fallen for."

"No, it's the kisses. If you want me to keep hanging around…" She cocked an eyebrow.

He obliged with another sweet but short kiss. "Don't try to get me in trouble, Foster. Clearly there are plenty of things we need to *talk* about so we know each other better." But he pulled her close for one last kiss. "I like saying goodbye to you before heading off to work," he whispered before releasing her. "See you at singles group tonight."

The kids slept until just after Anna, looking worn and rumpled, walked in at nine, almost like they sensed her arrival. She showered, dressed, and ate the continental breakfast in the room with the kids.

"How's Sophie doing this morning?" Jordan asked as Anna prepared to return to the hospital.

"A little better. She got her usual breakfast, and one of her favorite nurses stopped in to see her. Sophie's not one of her patients anymore, so that made Sophie's morning." Anna paused as Avery ran by, dressed in her pajama bottoms and summer top. "I got a text from Joelle this morning. She said she hasn't told her husband yet."

"What a relief that is."

Anna shot her a grateful look. "I know. Wish I'd known that yesterday. I'd have slept better. What are your plans for the day with the kids?"

"I thought I might get them outside. Would they like going to a park? A playground? Is Logan too old for that?"

"Take a soccer ball or something, and he's in. Avery too. When will you be back here?"

"After lunchtime, I'm sure."

"Okay. I'll pick up the kids sometime in the afternoon

so they can get time with Sophie." Anna pulled Jordan into a hug. "You have no idea what a huge help this is. Thank you."

How could she have stayed home, knowing all Cam and Anna and the kids were going through? "I'm happy to do it, Anna."

Anna released her and called towards the bedroom area. "Avery? Logan? I need to go."

The kids came running.

Anna said her goodbyes and told the kids to obey Jordan. They both hugged their mom, and she was off.

"So," Jordan said once the door was closed, "what do you guys want to do? Go to a park? Throw a football around? Play catch?"

Logan's eyes lit up. "I've got my soccer ball."

It'd been a long time since she'd played soccer. And it certainly wasn't her favorite. But Anna sure knew her son. "You like soccer, Avery?" she asked.

Avery nodded. "My daddy played soccer."

Okay then. Soccer, it was.

And Jordan would make sure she enjoyed it.

CHAPTER ELEVEN

That night they met in the parking lot, Cam having pulled in as she locked her car. "How do we let everyone know we're a couple?" he teased as they neared the church entrance. "Should I dip you and plant one on you? Right as we walk in the classroom?"

Oh, it was tempting. "I say we just be ourselves and see who's observant and who's not."

"Then you're expecting everyone to know before the night's out."

True. There was nothing like a church singles group for finding out who was dating whom. Even if it had been just two days.

The classroom was filling up. As they walked in, Cam raised an eyebrow at Jordan, a smirk on his face.

"I'm waiting," she teased him back.

The back rows were fairly full, so Cam picked end seats on the second row. He let Jordan go in before him, but before he could follow, Garrett scooted in between them. "Jordan, move down one. I'm gonna have to sit between you two and chaperone, I can tell."

And it was out.

Leave it to Garrett.

From the front row, Miska caught Jordan's eye and laughed. Dillan chuckled beside her.

Were they not going to help? "Garrett, don't you have a seat already?"

He leaned close to her and whispered. "Matt needs to know you're taken." He straightened. "Fine. But I'm watching you lovebirds."

Matt was back?

Cam sat beside her and laid his arm along the back of her chair. "Your brother," he said, giving his head a small shake.

If Matt even came over and tried to get her to meet him for dinner or coffee or anything—

"Hey." Cam's voice in her ear brought her back. "You okay?"

She flashed him a smile. If Matt was watching, she couldn't let him know she gave him any thought at all. Because she didn't. Not anymore. "I'm good."

He eyed her, clearly not quite believing her. "Anna told me you offered to watch the kids tomorrow too, but there's no need."

"They're going to spend the day at the hospital again?"

"This is their normal right now. Sophie needs to see them, and they need to see her too. Which means you get to go shoe shopping, finally."

"And you never told me how tall you are." She tried to lose herself in playful banter. "I still don't know if I can buy heels or not."

"I'm six foot. What are you?"

"Five ten."

He pretended annoyance. "We better have tall kids."

By the end of the study, Jordan had forgotten about Matt. But when the class was over and people milled around, talking, Cam stiffened.

She followed his gaze.

Matt Burcham walked toward her, his military haircut from his Marine days gone, but his shock of blond hair still looking as good as ever. *He* still looked good.

But that had no impact on her. Not anymore. His smile, those blue eyes—there was nothing there for her.

"Hey, Matt." Cam held out a hand, and Matt took it. "Good to see you."

No, it wasn't.

"What brings you back to town?"

Matt gave a nonchalant shrug. "Visiting the family. My parents' anniversary is tomorrow. Twenty-nine years."

"Wow. That's a nice long time."

Jordan tried not to smile at the emphasis Cam put on the words.

"Yeah, it is." Matt smiled her way. "Jordan. How are you?"

"I'm good." Why did she feel nervous? Before she knew it, she caught herself slipping her hand through Cam's, leaning into him—as if she were years younger and trying to make another guy jealous. "How's Indianapolis?"

"Well, it isn't Chicago, not food-wise, anyway. But the job's going well. The winter was much gentler. I can't complain."

"That's good."

And that was all she had to say—all she could *think* to say.

Cam took over and got Matt talking more about his job and life there.

As they talked, Jordan studied Matt's face. Back in high school, the first time they'd dated, she'd been so sure he was the one for her. Then he'd left for the Marines and hardly contacted her for four years. When he'd returned to the Midwest last summer, he'd wanted to pick up where they'd left off—no, where he'd tossed her aside—and she'd stupidly believed he was different. Older. Changed for the better.

When she'd left for her senior year of college, he'd disappeared from her life again. She didn't even know he'd taken a job in Indy until she came home for Thanksgiving. *Welcome back, Jordan. Matt doesn't live in Chicago anymore. Didn't tell you. Didn't send you his new address.*

But over Christmas he'd convinced her to go out with him while he was in town.

And then vanished again.

Before second semester midterms, Jordan had known she was done with him for good. But how she wished she could have made that clear to him before she was dating someone else. Before he thought she was on the rebound. Which had to be what he was thinking.

She left the guys to talk some more and hung out with Miska and two other friends. Even as she tried to lose herself in conversation, she couldn't help peeking at Cam and Matt, still talking.

What were they saying now that she was gone?

By the time Miska left with Dillan and her friends had said goodnight, Cam was talking to someone else—and Matt headed her way.

Jordan tensed.

He had that look in his eye that said he wasn't coming to shoot the breeze.

Not this time.

"Jordan, Jordan, Jordan," he said. "How's life really treating you?"

"Very nicely, actually."

He nodded like he didn't believe her. "It is, huh?"

"Better than the past year or so."

His smile said he'd understood her verbal jab. "You and Cam are a couple? Why?"

"What do you mean *why*? What's wrong with Cam?"

"Nothing's wrong with Cam, except no relationship ever lasts with him. He dates a girl for... what, two weeks? And then it's over—"

"Do you hear yourself?" Anger shook her voice. "Did he ever string them along? Make them think it was a serious thing and then leave them in limbo for days on end?"

He ducked his head. "Yeah, I know. I haven't... I've not been good to you."

"No, you have not."

"And I'm sorry. I really am, Jordan. You're the reason I

came home this week. I wasn't going to, but then I couldn't stop thinking about you."

"Please."

Her disgust stopped him cold.

"My guess, Matt, would be that you and some other girl down in Indy just ended things. That's why you were thinking about me—if you even were."

He shifted and looked away, his own face hardening. "You really think Cam will be around two weeks from now?"

"Yes."

"A month from now?"

"Matt."

"What if you're wrong?"

She had no worries about being wrong. Cam was the one for her, just like he knew she was the one for him.

"Meet me for dinner tomorrow. Or coffee. Let's catch up and see where things—"

"Absolutely not. I'd never go out with another man when I'm dating the man I love." The words slipped out, and she cringed. "I hate that you're the one who hears first that I love Cam." She clenched her fist. "I hate that."

"You think he loves you? You just started dating."

Cam might not have said the words yet, but she had no doubt as to his feelings. "And you think we had anything close to love?"

"Sure, we—"

"I had a crush on you, Matt. For years. But that's all it was. A crush." When would he get it? "And I'm over it now."

That bored look covered his face, the mask he wore when they argued. Yes, Matt had been fun to date, fun while he paid attention to her. But his attention span had been short.

Cam was different though.

Or he would be. This time. Wouldn't he? She was meant for him, and he was meant for her.

She shoved away the doubt that suddenly niggled in the corner of her mind. "I need to go. Congratulate your parents for me."

CHAPTER TWELVE

"Here's your shake." Cam handed Jordan the tall, cold glass filled with Oberweis's famous chocolate shake and sat at the counter beside her, his own shake in hand. They'd stopped by the ice cream shop after church, just to have a few minutes to themselves. "What did Matt have to say?"

She took a long sip before answering. "That you wouldn't be around in a month."

Jerk. "And here I was, being nice to him."

Jordan shrugged like it didn't matter, but she focused on the straw in her shake as she spoke. "Did he say anything to you?"

"About us dating? No."

"Good."

Was it? Matt should have challenged *him*, not Jordan. What was with the guy? Why did he play with her like that? There wasn't a better girl out there. Everything about Jordan was perfect—her candor, her sense of humor, her stability, her beauty, including that smile of hers that made him want to pull her close—

That smile of hers that was nowhere to be seen.

He inched his stool closer to hers. "You *do* know I'll be here in a month. Right?"

She looked up at him, her brown eyes revealing... what? Hurt? Doubt?

She doubted him? "Are you serious, Jordan? You believe him?"

"No." She fiddled with her straw again. "But..."

"But what?"

She sighed and pushed herself back from the counter. "I wish it *were* two weeks from now. A month from now. Cam, I *am*... nervous."

What did he say? He locked his jaws together. If he even opened his mouth right now—

"Don't be mad. Please."

"I'm not mad."

"Yes, you are. Your face is all tight. Your hands are clenched."

He relaxed the fist he hadn't known he'd made.

"I won't date Matt again because I know that, for whatever reason, he doesn't—didn't—take our relationship seriously. I wanted things to last with him, but he..."

So she'd still be with the guy, if he'd stuck around? "Did you love him?"

Jordan's big eyes were full of heartbreak. "I thought I did."

Awesome. He looked down at his shake, fiddled with the cold base.

"But I didn't. I told him that too. And I told him that I..." Her voice trembled. "I told him that I loved you."

Cam jerked his head up.

She was watching him, that doubt still on her face. What did that mean? Had she told Matt that and now wished she could take it back? "You said that?" He forced a chuckle from his suddenly dry throat. "I would have liked to have seen his reaction."

She looked away.

If he'd known all of this before Matt had left, he'd have cornered the guy and laid into him for trying to get back together with *his* girlfriend. For putting doubt in her mind about their future—when all the guy had done was yank her emotions around and make her think that no man would stick with her.

Jordan deserved so much better than that.

He reached for her hand, but when his fingers touched hers, she flinched. "Jordan, I'll be here. Not just a month from now but years from now."

She slipped her hand from his. "Thank you."

She didn't believe him. How could she not believe him? "You're upset with me? Why?"

"I don't like being a pawn between two guys."

"How'd I make you feel like a pawn?"

"Wishing you'd seen his reaction."

What was wrong with that? He loved Jordan. And she'd chosen him over an old boyfriend who'd seemed to have a real hold on her. Of course he wanted to see the guy's reaction to Jordan telling him that she loved—

Oh.

Oh, man, he was in trouble.

He slid his stool until it bumped up against hers, then wrapped both arms around her. She tensed in his arms, but he held her close. Didn't let her pull away. "Jordan."

She relaxed just enough to say she wasn't going to fight him.

"I'm a jerk too. I was so caught up in being happy that you told Matt how you felt about me that I didn't tell you how I feel about you. That I love you."

She still didn't react.

What was really going on here? Had he read her wrong? Why wouldn't she talk to him? "You know," he said, forcing playfulness into his voice, "technically you haven't told *me* you love me. You told *Matt* that you love me—"

"Cam, stop it." In a flash, she pushed out of his hold. "Is this a joke to you?"

"Of course not. I'm trying to get you to open up. It's not like you to keep your thoughts to yourself."

"You want to know what I'm thinking?" The fire was back in her eyes.

Which was both relieving and worrying.

"I'm thinking that I know I won't ever date Matt again because I know he won't be there for me. But he's right that you've been the same way. I've watched you date the new girl for a few weeks, then end it. How many times has that happened? How do I know that won't happen to me?"

"You're not the new girl."

"So what? You have this dating pattern, just like Matt does. And until we get past that pattern, I won't feel secure."

Anger fought understanding. "Tell me you were dealing with this before Matt talked to you."

"Of course not. He just reminded me of it."

"Right, because it makes me look bad. Because—I don't

know—he misses having you to come home to."

"Stop it."

"What? How am I wrong about that? Isn't that what he did? Even Dillan worried about that when he came back from the Marines."

"Stop it!" Her eyes filled. "I know I was stupid to keep taking him back. I know that!"

"That's not what I'm saying—"

"If you did that to me, Cam—"

"I won't." He grabbed her hands in both of his. "Jordan, listen to me. I won't. I'm telling you right now, I'm in love with you. With *you*. You're the woman for me."

She stilled. Listened.

"And I understand how what I've done in the past can make you doubt me. I wish you wouldn't, but I guess I understand it."

"You guess?"

He ignored that. "You talk about my dating pattern, but this *is* different. You're not the new girl. We've been getting to know each other for almost four years now, and I know more about you than any of the other women I dated. I never told them about Anna or Sophie. None of them knew a *thing* about my family. I've shared all of that with you. And"—he paused for effect—"I never told one of them that I loved them. Never. Never told them about… about my past. Never got into anything more than a casual relationship."

Head down, she wiped her cheek.

"Never even kissed them." He ducked to get a better look at her.

She wouldn't meet his gaze.

"Jordan, it makes me mad that he would go to you, knowing that we're a couple, and try to mess that up. I never thought Matt would do that. If I'd known before we left tonight, I would have let him have it. That's low. It is. I'd never do that to you. I *didn't* do that to you. Not when you came home from college a year ago and Matt showed up."

Finally, she looked up at him. "You were interested then?"

She sounded so insecure. "I was. But you were with Matt. And I wasn't going to step in and stir things up. I waited." Waited and prayed that his interest in Jordan would go away. And when it hadn't, that he'd know if he should pursue her or not when she got back from college.

Her gaze travelled across the emptying ice cream shop before returning to him.

He tried to read her expression. "I'd fight for you, Jordan. If I ever had to—if you suddenly thought we were done, I'd fight for you. For *us*."

Her voice was low. "Thank you."

But her words lacked feeling.

"I mean it, Jordan."

She raised her head and smiled tremulously at him. "I know. Thank you."

But something had happened tonight. Something had been damaged—and he didn't know what.

All he knew for sure was that he'd meant every word he'd said. He *would* fight for them.

CHAPTER THIRTEEN

"Look at this, Jordan. I think I've found bridesmaid dresses."

Jordan set aside her Panera sandwich and took the magazine from Miska. There were three dresses on the page. "Which one?"

"The one that's kind of a Jazz Age style."

The silvery blue dress was lovely. Tiny beads covered the dress in a subtle yet intricate pattern, adding a bit of sparkle and life to the light color. "Miska, I love it. It's gorgeous."

"Isn't it?"

"Is your dress like this?"

"Not really, but I think the two will go together. Mine's a modern take on lace, if that makes sense. More vibrant. It's got tiny cap sleeves and a diamond opening in the back. You'll have to come with me on my next fitting. It's pretty stunning."

Jordan handed the magazine back, smiling at her soon-to-be sister-in-law. "I bet you make the dress stunning."

"As long as Dillan thinks so."

"My word, girl, do you see him look at you? He'll definitely think so."

Miska grinned. "I can't wait. Three months, and it feels like it'll never get here."

"It'll get here." Where would she and Cam be in three months?

Miska leaned over the table. "I'd like to be really tactful and find some casual, normal way to fit this into conversation, but since I've only got twenty minutes left on my lunch break, I'm going to be nosy and jump right in. What did Matt say to you two Wednesday night?"

Jordan shrugged. "The usual. You know—hey, let's go out for dinner. By the way, Cam won't be here in a month."

Miska's mouth fell open. "Are you serious? He said that?"

"He did."

"What'd Cam say?"

Jordan groaned and covered her face with her hands. "Miska…"

"He doesn't know?"

"No. He knows. I told him." She dropped her hands and took a deep breath. "I told Matt that I love Cam."

Miska's face brightened. "You do?"

"I hadn't even told Cam yet. It made me angry that Matt heard it first. And then I told Cam later, and it was like he didn't even hear me say that it."

"Oh no. He didn't say it back? Jordan, you know the guy is crazy about you."

"He said it back. Eventually. But it felt like he realized he kind of had to." Jordan picked up her sandwich, studied it, then put it back down. "I don't know. It just hurt. I expected Matt to behave like that, you know? He dated me when it was convenient for him."

"Cam's not dating you because it's convenient."

With everything that had happened, she well knew that was true. "I know, but... The whole thing just made me mad. At both of them."

"You know you wouldn't be angry with Cam if it wasn't for Matt."

Leave it to Miska to be rational. "That's what Cam said too."

"He's right."

They both took another bite of their lunch, Miska checking the time on her phone.

"Miska, do you think this time with Cam it's different?"

"Yes."

"Why?"

"Well, I saw it over Christmas when you came home. Cam hung around you—us. At first I thought it was just Dillan he was hanging around with, but then I realized it was you. It'd be the four of us talking, Dillan and I would say goodnight and leave, and you two would still be there. Talking. Oblivious that we were leaving. We guessed then that he was interested in you." She shrugged. "But Matt came back for Christmas with his family, and that was the end of it."

Because Matt had dominated her time. She'd spent every spare moment with him. And Cam *had* faded into her background. Because she'd made it clear that Matt still had her heart.

If he'd wanted it.

Cam stiffening last night when he'd seen Matt... Jordan

closed her eyes. That little movement said so much more now.

Miska sipped her water, her eyebrows puzzled together. "What?"

"Do you think Cam was worried about me going back to Matt? When he showed up Wednesday?"

"You should ask him."

"Well." She felt silly now. "We kind of had an argument afterward."

Miska gave her a sympathetic look. "You're still together, though, right?"

"We are." She eyed the glittering diamond on Miska's finger. Dillan had been saving for that since January. He'd even taken Jordan to look at it before he bought it. Would Cam do something similar with Anna? "He told me he'd fight for me."

Miska melted a little. "That's sweet."

It was. And she'd been a moody, suspicious mess of a girlfriend. "I think I took it all wrong. I think I read Cam wrong."

"Are things between you bad?"

"No. But we didn't see each other yesterday. We've been together every day this week. Except yesterday."

"What about tonight? You got big Friday night plans?"

"He's going to call me when he gets off work."

Miska finished her salad, eyeing Jordan as she swallowed. "What do you think you should do? Are you in the wrong? Or is he? Or is nobody?"

Concern poked at her. "I think I might be."

"Then go see him. Fix it."

Where was she?

Peterson gripped the steering wheel, his fingers clenching and unclenching the leather. Two days he'd sat here, driven down Winters's street, up and down the street that connected to his. Two days.

And no Hannah.

Too bad Thomas wasn't around anymore. The man had either done a poor job or flat-out lied to him.

Peterson shook his head. He really should have made sure Hannah was where he'd been told she was before making sure Thomas wouldn't talk to anyone. Ever.

Too late now.

He leaned on the steering wheel, hoping the relaxation in the position would carry over into his thinking. *Breathe in, breathe out. Relax. Relax.*

Maybe it was time to take things into his own hands. After all, he had more worries back home to deal with.

He couldn't wait any longer, really. He had to decide what to do about his wife. *With* his wife, really.

He squeezed his eyes shut, pain dripping out of him. He couldn't lie to himself anymore. If he wanted to survive, it really *had* come to that. Two more women had to go.

Only then would he be safe.

A car sounded behind him, and Winters pulled past him, down the road, and into his driveway, parking in front of the garage. Alone, the guy stepped out of the car, holding his phone to his ear as he slowly climbed the stairs. Halfway up, he stopped as if listening to whoever was on the call.

Was it Hannah?

Winters ended the call and bounded up the stairs.

In his car, Peterson watched. What to do? How far to go?

He clenched his teeth. He'd come this far, literally and figuratively. If he stopped now, he'd lose everything.

He dragged his hand over his face. Everything he had left, anyway.

Chapter Fourteen

Jordan sounded better today. Happier. More like herself.

Cam set his phone on the charger in his bedroom. Even though she said she wanted to talk, the words didn't scare him. Wednesday had ended badly, and even their phone call on Thursday had been stilted. But now—she sounded so much better. Something had changed. Something good.

After he showered and dressed, he checked the time. He'd been able to leave work at a reasonable hour tonight, which was good, since he didn't have reservations anywhere. He grabbed his phone and stuffed it into his pocket. There was that really nice Chinese restaurant a few blocks away. That might be a good place for tonight.

The doorbell rang as he headed down the stairs.

Great. Just as he was heading out. Whomever it was, he didn't have time. He snagged his keys and wallet from the console table by the coat closet, then opened the door.

A fit, brown-haired man in a navy blue spring jacket—odd, considering how warm it was—stood there, head down, on the phone. He straightened and smiled. "Hello, Cameron."

This guy knew him? "Sorry. I don't…" No, he did know him. Broad jaw, lines on his face that said he'd spent too much time in the sun—

The man's free hand reached inside his coat.

As his face registered, tension poured over Cam. "Peterson?"

The man's smile broadened. He rushed the open door as his hand cleared his coat, aiming a black and yellow… gun?

Electricity charged through Cam, ramrodding every muscle, every limb, in his body. Completely rigid, he fell backward, yelling out—he hoped?—for it to stop. For the pain to quit—the electric punches that pounded incessantly—

He hit the floor with his tailbone, his head banging against the hardwood. And then—

Nothing.

At first, the worst thing about Cam being late was that she didn't know if this was typical of him or not. He'd said he'd be at her house by six. But at six fifteen…

Was something wrong? Had something happened?

At six thirty, she started calling him. Over and over.

He didn't pick up.

Alone at home, she paced the foyer, calling him then glancing out the windows by the front door to see if he was pulling in the driveway.

Nothing.

Was something wrong with his phone? Maybe calls weren't getting through. What about a text?

Her fingers flew across her phone. *Where are you? Are you okay?*

Two minutes later, her phone dinged. *Sorry. Something came up.*

Seriously? Why couldn't he have called her and let her know? Here she was, half-crazy with worry, the other half-ticked at him.

She texted back. *What happened?*

No reply.

Cam? Are you okay? Should I come over?

Her phone dinged again. *Yes. Thanks. Come over.*

Her shoulders relaxed at that. Whatever had happened, he wasn't ditching her. He still wanted her there.

So what had happened?

Sophie!

The name flashed through her, pulling fear and worry behind it. Something had to have happened to Sophie. Cam would never stand her up, unless something horrible had happened.

Had Sophie… died?

Jordan covered her mouth with her hand.

That had to be it—why he hadn't called her, wasn't answering his calls. He had to be with Anna and the kids.

And they all had to be a mess.

She grabbed her purse and keys and sent one last text as she headed to her car. *Is it Sophie?*

The answer came just as she started the engine. *Yes.*

Hurry. I'll leave the door open.

Hands shaking, she backed out of the driveway, praying that Sophie wasn't dead. That Cam and Anna would be okay. That she'd make it to Cam's house safely.

That everything would be all right.

CHAPTER FIFTEEN

For the last forty minutes, Cam had watched the clock on his bedside table, begging God to keep Jordan from his house. To give her a flat tire. To kill her engine. To put her in an accident.

Anything to keep Peterson from getting his hands on her.

"Cam?"

Her voice, just inside the front door, reached him faintly in his bedroom. Adrenaline ripped through him, and he strained against the ropes that bound his hands behind the chair. "Jordan! Run!"

His front door slammed. Scuffling sounded.

Jordan screamed, and something fell over.

No!

He panted in his chair, holding as still as he could to hear.

"That's enough. Stop fighting me."

A lone sob burst from Cam. Peterson had Jordan. The scum had Jordan. What would he do?

God, don't let him hurt her.

"Jordan!" Cam called, his heart drumming inside him. "Jordan, are you okay?"

Downstairs, Peterson's voice rumbled, his words indecipherable.

Jordan said something back.

Peterson barked at her, and footsteps thumped up the stairs.

Cam fought the ropes around his wrists again. They'd been loosening, but he was nowhere close to being free. His dizziness might be fading, but he had no idea how he'd feel once he was on his feet. He'd hit his head pretty good when he'd fallen. When the creep of a doctor had tased him.

Had he tased Jordan? It hadn't sounded like it. But she had to fight or they were both goners.

"Jordan, go!" he roared, head pounding. "Fight him! Push him! Go!"

Someone thudded against the stairway's walls.

Peterson cursed and Jordan cried out.

Cam kept yelling for her to fight, his words the only way he could help her. Tears fell down his cheeks. This guy could kill them. She had to get away. *Had* to.

"I said stop!" Peterson's voice rose over the sounds of a struggle. "That's enough. You want to make this worse? You get up now."

"Don't do it, Jordan—"

"Winters, you shut up!" Peterson bellowed.

Cam clenched his teeth.

What was that sound? Was Jordan crying?

If he could just get his hands on the guy— "Fight him, Jordan!"

Jordan stumbled into view.

No. Cam slumped in his chair.

Peterson was right behind her, gripping her upper arms, propelling her forward into the bedroom.

Hair disheveled, she glanced around, her gaze finally landing on him where he sat tied to a dining room chair in the far corner. She gasped. "Cam!" She tried to round on Peterson, her purse swinging from where it dangled on her forearm. "What did you do to him?"

He looked bad, huh? The guy had beat him up a good bit, trying to get Anna's location out of him. Hannah, actually. How strange it was to hear her real name again. But he'd taken the punches rather than give her up.

Peterson pushed Jordan deeper into the room and closed the door behind him. "He brought all that on himself. All he has to do is give me the information I want. That's all."

Right. Then Peterson would walk out and let them go free.

Not likely.

He'd been okay with that when it had just been him and Peterson. But Jordan… This changed everything.

One look in Peterson's eyes proved he knew it too.

Jordan rushed to him and knelt before his chair, her fingertips gliding across his face. "How badly are you hurt?"

"Not bad." Her fingers grazed a tender place on his cheekbone. Okay, that spot *did* hurt. "How are you?"

A tear trickled down her cheek, and she sent him a shaky smile. "I'll be okay."

He lowered his voice, trying to speak without moving his lips. "Tell me you called the police."

Her face fell.

So they were on their own.

"I'm so sorry, Cam."

No, he was sorry. Horribly sorry that Jordan was caught up in his nightmare. That she didn't know him enough to know that he'd never ignore her calls and instead text her back. If only they'd been dating longer... Maybe then she would have known something was seriously wrong. That he needed help, not her here, held captive with him.

"It's not pink," she said.

He frowned at her. "What?"

"Your bedroom. There's no pink."

A chuckle escaped. "No."

Her fingers slid across his temple, into his hair, around the back of his head.

As she came to what had to be a big lump on the back of his head where he'd hit the floor, he cringed. "Ow."

Her fingers eased up a bit, and she leaned around him to get a view, her purse sliding off her arm and onto the floor behind his chair. "What happened here?"

"He got tased," Peterson said, arms crossed from where he watched by the door. "If you want, I can do it again for you."

Jordan flashed a scalding glare over her shoulder. "No thanks."

He shrugged. "Might be up to you."

Jordan looked back at Cam, worry in her eyes.

He hoped his own didn't reflect it because no way did he want to go through that again. How long it had lasted, he didn't know because once he'd hit the floor so hard, he'd been out. And his head still hurt, still pounded. He had to have a concussion of some sort.

But he remembered enough to know that hitting the floor with his head hadn't been the worst of it.

He fought off a shudder.

She whispered something.

What? He scowled at her.

"Let me see if you're hurt anywhere else." She leaned closer to his face, examining the other side of his head, her back to Peterson across the room.

Cam held Peterson's glare as she continued to check his shoulder, his neck—

"Nail kit. Scissors," she whispered in his ear.

Cam froze. Where?

"What else did you do to him, Dr. Peterson?" She kept her gaze on Cam. "You've punched him in the face. I can see that. What else did you do?"

"What's it matter?" Peterson said. "All he has to do is tell me where Hannah is, and it stops."

He kept talking, but Jordan continued her pretend examination. "Purse. Behind you." She leaned around him, checking the side of his head, and braced one hand on the top of the chair. He heard something move behind him, then she shifted in front of him again. "I don't see any blood on that side." She leaned to the other side, and whispered. "Shelf behind you. In pocket."

If he could get to the scissors, maybe he could get through the rope and free himself. Free them both. Stop Peterson once and for all.

Jordan stopped her examination and stayed kneeling in

front of him. Her eyes filled. "I'm so sorry."

"Why are you apologizing? It's not your fault he got you too." His fingertips found her purse and followed the leather up to the open zipper across the top.

"No. For the other night. For not understanding how you might worry about Matt being back."

Worry about Matt? He frowned at her. Man, it was hard to concentrate on what she was saying *and* find his way into her purse. "What are you talking about?"

"I realized it was the first time Matt's been back since we started dating and that you might worry that—" She swallowed. "You know, that I might go back to him. Like I've done before."

But he hadn't worried about that. Not once. "No, Jordan. I trusted you." Completely.

His thumb braced the small purse while two of his fingers fumbled through paper and pens, her wallet, a cough drop—What did a nail kit feel like? Where was it?

Peterson approached. "Enough of this. What are you, a nurse?"

Cam held still, praying his body shielded the purse from Peterson's view.

The guy grabbed Jordan's arm and pulled her to her feet.

She squawked out a painful protest.

Cam bit his tongue, trying not to react, to do anything that would make Peterson realize how desperate he'd be to keep her safe.

What would he do if the man started hurting Jordan? No way could he give up Anna.

But he couldn't give up Jordan either.

Peterson shoved Jordan onto the edge of the bed, and she caught herself, staying upright. "I assume," Peterson said, sending Cam a quick glance of hate, "that you also know where Hannah is. Why don't you tell me so we can all go home?"

Jordan stared up at him. "Does Joelle know you're here?"

Peterson jerked his head back toward Jordan at his wife's name.

"Wait." She pointed at him. "*You* sent that text from Joelle."

What text?

"You did, didn't you? What's happened to your wife? Is she okay? Did you kill her too? Just like that nurse?"

Peterson took a step back, eyes narrowing with anger. With hate.

Dread filled Cam. How could she let Peterson know that they knew? What was she doing?

"Why'd you kill her? Was she going to tell Anna that the baby didn't belong to you and Joelle? That you gave her the wrong embryo?"

"I didn't give her the wrong embryo!" Peterson barked. "I knew *exactly* what I was doing."

Cam dug through the purse. His fingers brushed against a zipper in the purse's wall.

"Your wife's not the mother. You're not the father—"

"Oh, I'm the father." Peterson nodded emphatically. "I made sure *I* was the father."

"Then who…"

The zipper gave beneath his trembling fingers, slowly moving sideways.

"Wouldn't you like to know?" Peterson snapped his gaze Cam's way.

Cam froze.

"You got any guesses, Winters?"

"No."

Peterson reached for Jordan.

Cam's heart jumped. "I mean, I thought maybe the baby was Tony's. Tony and Anna's. That she was pregnant when she went in for the procedure and you never told her."

"That wouldn't have worked. Tony was too dark. Joelle would have known we weren't the parents." He gave a humorless laugh. "If only Hannah *had* been pregnant. We would have looked elsewhere for a surrogate. And none of this would have happened."

"You wouldn't say that if you knew Sophie." He slipped a finger inside the pocket. "She might not have been perfect in your eyes, but she's exactly the way she's supposed to be. She *is* absolutely perfect."

Peterson shook his head. "Really, Winters? She had Down's. That's what the test showed. You call that perfect?"

He raised his chin. "Absolutely."

"Fine then. If it's worth getting beat up for. Tased over. Watching your girlfriend go through all that too. Then I guess you're right."

A whimper bubbled out of Jordan.

"No!" The word burst out before he could contain it. He jerked forward, and the purse tilted with him. He grabbed it with every finger in his weary hand, losing the pocket. "No. Please. She's not part of this."

Peterson pulled the taser out of his coat pocket. "What's

your name, honey? Jordan? Is that right?"

She cowered before him, her eyes trained on the gun. "Yes."

Cam held his breath, his fingers reaching back into the pocket.

"She's real pretty, Winters. And there are so many ways I can hurt her. Is that what you want?"

His voice trembled. "No."

Peterson raised the taser. Pointed it at Jordan. "Where's Hannah, Winters?"

Jordan tried to backpedal across the bed.

Cam couldn't help himself. "Please don't," he begged. "Please. Don't hurt her."

The taser fired.

Jordan jerked horizontal across the bed, legs jerking, neck arching.

"No!" Cam tried to shove himself to his feet, managing instead to knock the chair into the bookcase. "Stop it! Peterson! Stop!"

The tick-tick-tick of the taser lasted another second. Another. Another.

And all Cam could hear was himself crying out, sobbing, begging the man to stop. "I'll tell you!"

The taser silenced.

With a sudden gasp, Jordan slumped across the bed, her breath coming hard.

"Jordan!" Tears streamed down his face. "Are you okay?"

Slowly she pushed herself up, shaky, weak.

He knew how that felt—her muscles drained, exhausted.

"I'm all right," she finally said. But she looked terrified.

Her gaze pleaded with him, fear fighting with exhaustion. "Cam. Don't tell him."

What?

"You can't tell him."

He knew that. And he'd never tell Peterson. Never. But it had worked this one time, getting Peterson to stop hurting the woman Cam loved.

How would he stop Peterson the next time?

Or did he even have any more taser cartridges?

"Jordan. The wires! Get them off—"

She jerked the prongs free from where they'd attached.

Peterson watched, bemused. "You think that will stop me, Winters? I've got all night. And all weekend. No one's going to miss you tomorrow. What plans did you have? Spending the night with this one? Spending tomorrow with her? Who's going to notice that either one of you is gone?"

The scissors. The nail kit. Memory returned, reminding him why he had Jordan's purse in such a tight grip. He worked his finger back into the pocket. "People are looking for us right now. We had plans. With friends."

Peterson laughed. "Right. I'm not worried."

Cam's fingers slid across something thin and plastic. The nail kit!

"What was it like watching that, Cameron? Knowing *exactly* what it felt like?"

He slid the kit open. *Focus*, he told himself. Couldn't listen to this guy. Everything depended on him getting those scissors. Cutting himself free.

"You know, you kinda got lucky that you fell and hit your head. You missed a good three or four seconds of your tasing. But not your girlfriend here. She felt it all. How was that, Jordan? Hmm? You like that?"

Something sharp poked the tip of his finger. He swallowed, carefully grasping the metal point with his fingertips. He tugged.

The scissors inched forward.

"You want more, Jordan?"

Cam froze. Searched Peterson's face.

Peterson popped the cartridge off the front of the taser. He tossed it onto the bedside table and reached into his coat again. "Bought myself the nicest taser I could a couple of years ago." He waved it toward Cam. "You know, self-defense. Can't be too safe anymore."

What did the guy want? Congratulations?

"Nice thing is that this model comes with six cartridges."

No. No no no.

Peterson pulled his hand out of his pocket, another awful yellow cartridge displayed for Jordan to see. "Just so you know, Jordan, I've only used two cartridges. Four left." His grimace of a smile was pure evil. "You know where Hannah is, Jordan? Hmm?"

Jordan's chest rose and fell rapidly.

Don't tell him, Cam prayed. *Please don't tell him.*

"Why do you want her?"

The scissors slipped free of the plastic.

"Why do I want her? Seriously?"

Cam worked his fingers down the scissors' shaft until he could spread them open.

"Guess he hasn't told you everything, huh?" Peterson glared at Cam again, and Cam held himself still. "She stole my kid. Ran away with her."

"That baby wasn't yours."

"Yes, she was!" He waved the gun at Jordan's face. "I made sure of that. That baby was mine, and I had every right to demand she abort it—"

"Your own child?"

Cam dragged the tiny scissors across the thin rope. The tip nicked his wrist, and he flinched, readjusting his hold.

He couldn't afford to drop these.

"Joelle agreed with me. We hadn't come all this way— spent all that money—for a messed-up kid."

When he got his hands on this man…

"How do you know that? You've never seen her."

"I saw the test. Read the results."

"What if you're wrong?"

Beneath the scissors, the rope gave a bit.

Cam yanked his wrists sideways.

The rope gave a little more.

Come. On.

"You know what? Enough of this." Peterson yanked Jordan up.

She yelped as he forced her to her feet.

Peterson spun her around, made her face Cam. "You want her fried again?"

Jordan squeezed her eyes shut as tears escaped down her face.

Cam fought back his own.

"She's not on the bed this time. She'll hit the floor. Or the edge of the bed. Your dresser. Something. Might be a whole lot worse than what happened to you. See, that's what they say is the worst part about being tased. Not the pain. That stops when the taser stops. No, the worst part is the fall. That's where the real injury happens. And this time I don't plan on catching—"

Jordan jerked her arm free, turned, and shoved him.

Cam dug the scissors into the weakening rope. The point rammed into the pad of his thumb, and out of instinct, he released the scissors.

They clanked against the floor at the same time that Peterson dropped the taser to corral Jordan.

Cam strained against the rope.

It crept apart. More. More.

"Cam!" Jordan screamed. She fought Peterson still.

He grabbed one of her wrists and fumbled for her other arm.

The rope gave.

And Cam flew out of the chair, sending it flying. Reached Peterson in two strides. He pushed Jordan to one side while grabbing Peterson's throat with his right hand, the one with blood on it.

Peterson's eyes widened.

Jordan fell back against his bed.

Cam's momentum took him and Peterson to the wall. They crashed there together, and the tall dresser beside them rattled, a picture frame toppling over.

Peterson yanked Cam's hand from his throat, and Cam's muscles, still weak from the taser, let him. The man swung at him, a sorry punch that just clipped his jaw.

But he'd left himself exposed.

Cam put everything he had behind his own shot to Peterson's stomach.

The man oofed over.

Cam knocked him to the ground.

While the man gasped for air, Cam straddled him, forcing the man's arms behind his back.

Beside him, Jordan offered him the rope.

A much smaller rope now.

He took it, looking up at her, his chest heaving, arms weary. Ready to fall to his sides. But somehow he mustered the strength to tie up the man who'd taken so much from so many.

Not until Jordan knelt beside him and wrapped him in her arms did he realize what a mess he was. He fought himself for control, only to rest his head on her shoulder and give in to the fear he'd struggled against. "I'm so sorry," he whispered into her hair.

"For what?"

"For letting him hurt you."

She pushed him up, shook her head at him. "You fought for me, Cam. Look at you." She held up his blood-stained hand. "You fought for me. And Anna. And Sophie."

How could he not? He cupped her cheek, brought her face to his, and kissed her. Slowly. Gently. Thankfully.

She kissed him back, her lips more intense than his.

Peterson writhed beneath him, and Cam pulled back enough to check his hold on the man.

"Are you going to send me home?" Jordan asked.

"No." He couldn't help a smile. "Not yet. 'Cause this time your dad and brothers *will* kill me."

CHAPTER SIXTEEN

It took time—weeks, actually, for all the details to come out.

Sometime after Anna had fled to Michigan, Dr. Peterson decided to let her and the baby girl he didn't want, go. So long as he never heard from her again.

But then Anna had called Joelle, knowing she'd not completely agreed with her husband on what to do about Sophie, asking her to consider being tested to see if she could be the match the little girl, suffering with leukemia, needed.

Peterson had overheard the call and knew that what he'd done in his own office—years ago, after his usual hours—was about to come out.

The nurse he'd blackmailed back then into helping him had seemed malleable at the time. No threat whatsoever. She'd helped him retrieve Anna's eggs under the pretense of implanting an embryo. He'd seen Anna's kids. They were healthy, good-looking, strong. And Anna's coloring wasn't too far off from his own.

No one would ever know. Not even his wife, who would

never, ever be able to conceive a child.

Not that she'd find out, if he had a say in it. The news would devastate her.

But Anna could spare her eggs. That was done under the guise of implanting a first embryo that he'd later say hadn't taken. Once enough time had passed for that, it was time to put the real one in. His and Anna's.

And it took.

But then had come the test results. Down Syndrome. A less-than-perfect child. He couldn't let that happen. Not when it had to be Anna's fault that this child was damaged. No way would he raise it. Or pretend to love it. Or provide for it.

No. The child needed to go.

The news spread throughout his office—how sad it was that after so many years of trying that Dr. and Mrs. Peterson's baby had Down Syndrome. Of course they'd abort and try again. But so sad. To be only a few months away…

His nurse had decided Anna needed to know.

And he needed to stop her.

That had been the deep, dark step that led him to doing whatever it took to keep it all a secret. To keep his practice. To keep his wife. To keep his freedom.

But one sinister choice led to another. After talking to Anna about not being a match, Joelle had confronted him with the news that she couldn't be the mother. Peterson, loathe to go as far with her as he'd done with the nurse, had locked her in their basement. With food. With water.

But still. His own wife.

Cam couldn't fathom it.

She'd escaped the same night Peterson had attacked them, a neighbor chasing a dog through her yard having heard her cries for help.

The body of the private investigator Peterson had hired showed up the next day. He'd been hit in the head with something hard. A tire iron, Peterson finally admitted.

Two people dead. Two more who might have ended up dead. Certainly three if Peterson had found Anna because Anna was the proof of what he'd done. The proof that he'd stolen her eggs and had used them to create his child. If he'd found a way to kill Anna—and not be suspected in her death—no one would ever, ever know what he'd done over five years ago.

But he hadn't found her. He hadn't—and now, at long last, Anna could live a normal life again.

Wrong finally *had* been righted.

The maternity test Anna and Sophie took proved they were indeed mother and daughter. That Sophie was Cam's biological niece after all. His parents' actual grandchild.

Cam left his parents a voicemail, letting them know.

There was no reply.

Not through the summer while he and Jordan continued to date. Not through the chemo and radiation week leading up to Sophie's transplant after a stranger had turned out to be an excellent match. Not through her slow but steady recovery.

And not through weeks of Garrett play-threatening— Cam hoped?— to tase him again if Jordan so much as stubbed her toe. Not through Cam listing his house and looking for something new—with Jordan's input—so he wouldn't have to walk past that bedroom every day and remember what had happened to them both.

He was ready to start over. To build a life with Jordan. A really nice, long, boring-as-dirt life.

"So. Dude." Garrett cornered him as Miska and Dillan's rehearsal dinner ended and people were heading to the church. "When's your closing again?"

"Tuesday. Are you coming to help me move?"

Garrett spread his hands, looked down at his expensive pants and shirt. "Do I look like I do my own moving?"

"Come on, man. Dillan will be on his honeymoon. Jordan can't help because you'll go all *Princess Bride* torture on me if she breaks a nail. And Matt might have moved back, but I do not want any help from him."

Grinning, Garrett clapped him on the shoulder. "Well then. Let me know how the move goes." He turned and walked away.

Cam watched him go. Maybe marrying into the Foster family wasn't all he'd thought it would be. Outside of getting Jordan, anyway.

Garrett glanced over his shoulder—and laughed. "Dad and I'll be there whenever you want. Let us know."

"Thanks." Yeah, Garrett as a brother-in-law was going to be… interesting.

The best part about the rehearsal wasn't that Miska and Dillan were getting married but that Cam got to walk down the aisle with Jordan. Pretty cool how that had worked out.

From his seat on the auditorium's front row, Cam listened to the wedding coordinator telling the bridesmaids where to stand. Miska's maid of honor, Tracy, was first with Jordan right behind her, and other bridesmaids following. Garrett was Dillan's best man with Cam right behind him.

They took their places on the stage while the coordinator stepped back to make sure it looked right. Cam looked past Dillan and Miska—who held hands and talked intimately, a huge smile lighting Miska's face—to Jordan directly opposite and, like him, two steps down from the bride and groom.

Pretty sweet that he'd have a perfect view of her tomorrow throughout the ceremony.

She smiled at him, and Cam raised his eyebrows. *Marry me*, he mouthed.

What? she asked.

Marry. Me.

A playful smile curved her lips, even as she rolled her eyes and tapped the bare ring finger on her left hand.

Yeah. Details. But he was working on that. Once Dillan and Miska were back from their honeymoon, he'd ask Jordan for real. Make it official.

They practiced walking off the stage, up the aisle, and out to the church's foyer.

Jordan slid her hand from where it curled around his bicep down to his hand. "You know," she said, "you keep randomly asking me to marry you like that, and I'm not gonna believe you when you're serious."

"Oh, you'll believe me." Cam stepped aside for Miska's

dad to join her for the walk down the aisle. "You'll know when it's the real thing."

"How?"

Because he'd probably be a bit of a mess himself. He knew it.

"Cam?"

See? He was starting to lose it now. What was wrong with him this summer? He cleared his throat. "You sure you want me? An old guy who's already getting emotional about everything? How bad am I going to be when I hit forty?"

Jordan leaned into him and planted a kiss on his lips.

Cam closed his eyes and cradled her against him.

"Hey, hey, hey," Garrett called from somewhere beyond them.

They broke apart to laughter from the rest of the bridal party, and Cam sent Garrett the evil eye.

"What? You're kissing my sister."

Yes, and Garrett needed to get used to it. Cam kissed her again, then held her close. "What is he going to say when we have kids?"

Jordan laughed as she slipped out of his arms.

They prepared for the walk down the aisle, and Cam tried not to think too far ahead to when it would be their turn.

Why?

Because it was Miska and Dillan's turn now.

Because Jordan deserved to be loved. Cherished. Honored.

Because they both were worth doing it right.

Dear Reader,

Thank you so much for reading *Taken* and for spending time with me, Cam, and Jordan. If you've read *Kept* already, I hope you enjoyed revisiting that world and those characters and getting peeks into Miska and Dillan's life together. This book was a bit different in style from what I normally write, but I hope to do more full-length novels for *Kept* characters down the road. Just waiting for the right idea to come together. Details, details! Right?

In the meantime, I've started a new book series about second chances. Like *Kept*, the Chicago Wind series deals with characters who are facing hurts and tough decisions, all while working to grow as a Christian. In *Homestands*, a professional athlete stumbles across his ex-wife, the son she hid from him, and the rare opportunity to right his wrongs; but a secret from the past threatens attempts to repair their shattered relationship. I thoroughly enjoyed Mike and Meg's story and hope you love it too. Keep reading for a sneak peek at the first chapter!

I do love hearing from you, reader friend, so feel free to get in touch with me either through my website or my Facebook page. I'd love to talk with you. And please subscribe to my newsletter to find out when more books are coming out.

Until we meet again,
Sally Bradley

PS: Don't forget to keep reading for a peek at *Homestands!*

Homestands

Chicago Wind, book one

When baseball star Mike Connor stumbles across his ex-wife six years after their divorce, he's stunned to find that she's the mother of a kindergartner who wears his jersey. And shares his last name.

The last thing Meg Connor wants is to be around Mike. After all, he was the one who hurt and abandoned her. But she can't deny him—or their son—time together to build a relationship, which means Mike is around too often, reminding her of why she fell in love with him so long ago. If only she could forget their past... The painful and the good.

Between their guilt and closely held hurts, Meg and Mike struggle against each other, their feelings, and God as they fight their own desires for the future, a future that might never happen when the past that tore them apart collides with their present.

Chapter One

The end came, as it nearly always did, when his thoughts were elsewhere, his focus on other things. When life seemed okay, if not good.

This time he was staring at the years-old picture he held

of himself with Meg when he realized that someone had, several seconds ago, sat down beside him on the bed.

And that it could only be Sara.

It was too late to hide the picture.

But he did anyway.

Sara drew her eyes slowly to his, her lips pressed together. "This isn't working, is it?"

"I just found it. I was packing and—"

"Mike Connor." She laughed and eased to her feet with the same calm reaction she gave all of his jokes. "Who do you think you're lying to here?"

"No one. I'm not lying."

"Well, you're definitely not lying to me." She turned in front of the bathroom doorway and watched him.

He tried not to squirm.

Her crossed arms said control, not self-preservation. She pursed her lips. "I've seen this coming for a while, you know."

He played dumb. "Seen what coming?"

"The end of us."

"Sara." He forced all the emotion and love he could into her name. "I told you. I was packing and I found it."

"Why is it even here, Mike? You brought everything in this place six weeks ago when you came down for spring training. If this were your house, then maybe—maybe—I could see you stumbling across it."

He glanced around, his gaze finally landing on the black Samsonite peeking from the bottom of the open closet. "It must have already been in a suitcase."

"Right." She leaned against the doorjamb, sending him

a sad smile. "You're not over her."

"Come on." He laughed. "Don't tell me you never think about past relationships."

"How often are we talking, Mike? Why do I get the feeling that every relationship you've had has ended this way? I know what I'm talking about—you're not over her. You need to see her."

"No. Nope." His pulse sped just a bit at the idea. He hadn't seen Meg in over six years. Six long years in which every relationship fizzled under the memory of what he'd thrown away.

But Sara was right about one thing—the two of them had been over for a while. Back in February he'd been eager to leave her in freezing Chicago and hightail it to sunny Arizona. Nothing but the team and baseball—until a week ago when she'd come down to stay with him over spring break. He rubbed his eyes, suddenly worn out and longing for sleep.

"Do you realize you're still sitting on the bed? That your hand is still on her picture? You haven't even bothered getting up to persuade me to stay."

Wow. He studied the pattern of the carpet. No rebuttal came to mind.

But the thought of going back to his massive home and finding it empty of everything Sara was depressing. He forced himself to stand, his knees creaking, and walked across the bedroom to her.

She stayed where she was, her eyes on him.

He pulled her into his arms, and she let him, even though her arms stayed folded in front of her.

They really were done.

His throat tightened. There was so much he should say, but his voice would betray him. And what was he really emotional about this time? Was he sorry to see Sara go? Or just sorry that he'd be alone?

Again.

Sara sighed as she moved out of his arms and stepped around him.

He turned, watched her walk to the nightstand.

Her straight brown hair hung down her back in a thick, soft ponytail. She loved her hair, and he'd lied and told her he thought it was beautiful too.

But it was always dark, honey-blonde hair he loved. Meg's long, wavy hair.

Sara pulled something from her planner and palmed it.

"What?" he asked. "You've got an ex-husband you're going to show me?"

"Stop it. I want you to go see her."

"This is dumb, Sara. I don't even know where she is or what—"

She held out her hand. A business card rested in her palm.

Mike stared at the card. She had to be kidding. "No."

"Take it, Mike."

He couldn't.

A moment later it was in his hands. *Meghan Connor Designs.* He read the raised lettering, his heart thudding inside him. This couldn't be.

"She's half an hour from you, Mike. From either home."

Half an hour.

"She's an interior designer. Another teacher recommended her when we looked into hiring someone. I hear she's good."

"She's very good."

"Yes." She cleared her throat. "Well."

Half an hour away? They'd been in Texas when they'd divorced, and she'd vanished so fast. He'd been traded to Chicago just over a year ago, fresh off another break-up, Meg on his mind.

For the last year she'd been half an hour away.

"I'll get into O'Hare around six tonight. By the time you get back to Chicago on Sunday, I'll be out of your place." Sara picked up her things as she talked—a perfume bottle, her iPad, her flat iron, and makeup bag. She shoved them one after another into her carry-on, the first sign that this hurt. "I'll mail you my keys. You'll get them next week."

Always on top of things. Always ready for anything. "Where will you go?"

"I guess I—" She stopped her stuffing and froze over the bag. Her ponytail slid over her shoulder and covered his view of her face.

He studied Meg's business card.

A moment later she sniffed and zipped her bag closed.

Mike looked up.

She was wiping her nose.

She jabbed a finger at him. "You go see her. You find out if there's anything left there. You hear me?"

"Sure." Not likely.

"And after all that, if there's nothing left between you two—" Three quick steps, and she was in his arms.

He held her while she shook against him.

But just as quickly, it was over and she pushed herself back. "If it ever really ends between you two, then you call me. Okay?"

"Okay."

It wouldn't happen. Sara was already his past. There was no going back.

He looked beyond her at the picture lying on the bed. Not even Meg would take him back.

BOOKS BY SALLY BRADLEY

Kept—Can a woman with a messy past
find love with a good man?

Chicago Wind
Homestands (book one)—A professional athlete stumbles across
his ex-wife, the son she hid from him, and the rare opportunity
to right his wrongs; but a secret from the past threatens their
attempts to repair their shattered relationship.

About the Author

Sally Bradley has been a fiction lover for as long as she can remember—and has been fascinated by all things Chicago (except for the crime, politics, and traffic) for almost as long. A Chicagoan since age five, she now lives in the Kansas City area with her pastor/cop husband and their three children, but she and her family get back to Chicago when they can for good pizza and a White Sox game. A freelance editor and former president of her local writing chapter, Sally has won a handful of awards for her first book, *Kept,* and another, soon-to-be-released *Shelf Life*. Visit her online at sallybradley.com.